SKATING BACK TO YOU

A HOCKEY HEARTS / ON STAGE ROMANCE

JEFF ADAMS

BIG GAY
Media

ONE

DIXON

"Mr. Cliff. Good evening. It's wonderful to see you." Miss Julia handed me a program. She'd worked the aisle leading to my season ticket seats at the Koch Theater for nearly every performance I'd attended since I'd arrived in the city over the summer. No matter how many times I'd asked her to call me Dixon, she wouldn't do it.

I gave a single nod and a broad smile. "Good to see you too, Miss Julia. I'm glad I could catch this show before I head out tomorrow."

"Oh yes." She beamed a bright smile. I'd learned early on that the bigger her smile, the more I'd enjoy the performance. "It's an incredible production."

"Good to know. You've never led me wrong." Miss Julia reminded me of my grandmother. I knew from talking to her during intermissions that she'd worked here for decades. The stories she had about the people and shows she'd seen were captivating. I'd met her the first time I'd come here to see the New York City Ballet perform. She'd recognized me from the Empire even though I'd only just arrived for training camp. She knew her hockey.

"I trust you can find your seat?" She always asked that question.

And I always responded the same. "Yes, ma'am."

Tonight I was here solo since I needed to catch *Ballet Strong,* which was starting a weeklong engagement. Sometimes friends came along since I had two seats, but tonight I'd kept it simple since I had an early flight out with the team. There was no way I could miss a show featuring male dancers doing a mix of traditional male solos along with new numbers choreographed specifically for the show.

I made my way down to the first row. I enjoyed sitting in the first balcony, and securing seats here and at the adjacent Metropolitan Opera House had been among the first things I'd done when I knew I'd be moving to New York. My parents loved theater and dance and they had brought me up on arts programs on PBS and the occasional live performance when something interesting had played in the area. I hadn't always understood what I saw in those programs, but watching people move to music had captured my imagination—and still did today.

I slid into the row, saying, "Excuse me" as I went. A young boy was playing on his phone to my right while the seat to my left was empty since I hadn't brought anyone.

"Whoa." The boy stretched the word out while keeping his voice down. His parents had clearly taught him how to behave in a theater. "You're Dixon Cliff."

His eyes were wide.

"Hi. Yes, I am."

"I'm so sorry." His mom looked at me and then at him. "Evan, you shouldn't be bothering him."

I shot her a smile. "It's okay." I turned my attention to Evan. "It's nice to meet you, Evan."

"I didn't know hockey players liked ballet."

Not the first time I'd heard that. "I always have. Dancers are some of the most incredible athletes. And the stories they can tell without words are amazing."

He shrugged. "I guess the pirate show was pretty cool. They even had swords."

"*Le Corsaire*," Evan's mom offered.

"That's one of my favorites."

"My sister likes everyone falling in love." On the other side of his mom sat a girl who looked a year or two older than Evan. She ignored our conversation in favor of reading the program. Beside her was an empty chair.

"Can't wait to tell everyone I saw you. Dad'll flip too when he comes back. Mom?" He held the phone out to her. "Can you take a picture of us?"

"Evan, I'm sure he'd rather not."

Being stuck between a parent and child wasn't my favorite place. She clearly wanted to set boundaries with him, but I didn't mind taking a picture either. Evan looked at her and I took the moment to mouth *It's fine* to her so she knew.

"Is it okay with you?" Evan turned back to me.

His mom gave a quick nod with a quiet "Thank you."

"Sure." I leaned next to him and he got a little closer. His mom snapped a couple of pictures.

"You're going to bring home wins on the road, right?"

"That's the plan."

"Dad, look who's sitting next to me." Evan was a little louder and his mom put a hand on his shoulder.

I heard "Excuse me" coming from behind me and stood to find someone who was unmistakably Evan's father.

"Dixon Cliff," I said, holding out my hand.

"Andrew Braxton." We shook. "And apparently you've met Evan."

"Yes, I have. We talked a little about what he likes to see in a ballet."

Andrew chuckled. "I'm sure it involved pirates. I hope he didn't disturb you."

"Not at all."

The lights flashed, indicating the performance would start in a few moments.

"Evan, make sure you don't bother him during the show."

Out of the corner of my eye, I saw him nodding vigorously.

"Good to meet you, Dixon. And thanks." Andrew gestured at Evan, who was turning off his phone, then headed to his seat on the other side of his family.

Once I'd taken off my coat and settled in my seat, I opened the program to take a quick scan. I liked to read everything before the performance started, but I'd have to settle for the lineup for the evening and read the rest at intermission.

The name of the dancer performing a solo from *Swan Lake* stopped me.

Oscar Salazar.

Could it be?

I flipped through the booklet looking for pictures. Even though he was all grown up, I recognized him immediately—the kind expression, an energy in his eyes that relayed eagerness, and the dark, curly hair. Before I could flip to his bio, the lights faded and the conductor walked to his podium in the orchestra pit.

Anticipation skyrocketed at the thought of seeing Oscar dance for the first time in nearly twenty years.

When the lights came up on stage, there were eight men sitting and doing stretches on the floor. The orchestra sounded as if they were warming up, although the conductor was guiding them.

My gaze went right to Oscar, the third from the right, as he stretched out to touch his toes. I couldn't look away as he stood and slowly raised his left leg and brought it up to the side of his head.

Damn.

His picture didn't fully capture how handsome he'd become. The light blue sleeveless shirt he wore popped against his light brown skin. His strong arms were on full display, and as he went through his warm-up, it became even more apparent how fit he was.

Suddenly the music exploded into "The Rumble" from *West Side Story* and the dancers broke into movement across the stage. Controlled chaos was the only term that came to mind. They settled into a dance battle, calling out to each other to do something bigger, bolder.

Each performer had their own spectacular flair. I tried to take it all in, but my attention drifted back to Oscar. He vibrated with energy, constantly moving even when he wasn't center stage. It reminded me of being ready for anything in a face-off.

The energetic medley of *West Side* songs continued while the dancers gave the audience a taste of what they each brought. At the end, they formed a line at the front of the stage, reminiscent of *A Chorus Line*.

After that, it felt like an eternity until Oscar returned to the stage to dance Prince Siegfried's solos from *Swan Lake*. This was the number that had caught my eye. I'd seen a few versions of the ballet over the years and this was choreography I'd never seen before. He owned the stage with a perfect combination of power and grace. Not until he finished did I realize how far forward I'd moved in my seat or that I'd held my breath for the final set of twirls and leaps.

I restrained myself from a standing ovation for just the third number, although I added to the audience's thunderous applause.

The show proceeded with incredible dance after incredible dance. Oscar appeared in another two ensemble pieces. He might as well have been out there solo, though, for as much attention as I paid anyone else.

After not appearing in the next three dances, he returned in a pool of light on the far left while another dancer was on the far right. I didn't recognize the beautiful music that accompanied them. They moved separately for a time but then closed the space between them.

In breathtaking starts and stops, it clearly became the story of a relationship that moved from friends to lovers. The pas de deux blew me away. I'd never seen one featuring two men and the strength they exuded, lifting and moving each other, exhilarated me. I wiped away a tear and took a deep breath as my chest vibrated from the emotionally charged story they told.

The dance continued, telling the story of a life lived. The longer it went, the more I couldn't control my emotions. Tears flowed freely as the music's last notes faded along with the lights. Oscar knelt over the other dancer, who lay still on the stage.

The audience erupted in applause. I sat still, unable to even join in. The dance would've evoked an emotional response no matter what, but seeing Oscar performing that left me profoundly moved. And if act one ended with that, I couldn't imagine what act two had in store.

The house lights came up on an empty stage.

"Mr. Cliff, are you okay?" Evan asked as I wiped my eyes.

I couldn't find my voice, so I looked over and nodded.

"Evan, he just needs a minute." His mom spoke quietly as I tried to get myself under control. She offered a tissue and I took it.

"Thank you," I managed to say without a voice crack.

"It was amazing," she said softly.

"Yes, it was."

"Come on, Evan," his dad said, "let's get you and Lizzie a cookie."

I stared at the stage and dabbed at my eyes. Oscar had come a long way from the recitals I'd seen him in.

Once I got the tears under control, I got up to stretch my legs and get water.

"What did you think?" Miss Julia asked as I emerged into the lobby.

"I'm not sure I have the right words." I held up the balled-up tissue.

She nodded. "I watch that last number every night. It's so good."

"Is there a way to get a message backstage? I'd like to see one of the dancers afterward, if that's possible."

"Of course. I can take one to the stage door to pass on."

"That would be amazing." Of course, I had no pen or paper, so that complicated things a bit.

"Here." Miss Julia passed over a pen and a small pad she produced from her jacket pocket.

"Thank you."

It only took a moment to compose the message.

O-man!
No fair making me cry!
I'd love to see you after the show if you're free. I'll come to the stage door.
- Dix

I tore the page out, folded it in half, and wrote Oscar's name on it.

"Thanks, Miss Julia. I haven't seen Oscar since we were kids and now to see what he can do..." I trailed off to avoid tearing up again.

"How wonderful. I'll make sure this gets to him. You know where the stage door is, right?"

"I do. Yes."

Chimes sounded, which meant that intermission would end in five minutes.

"I'm going to get some water," I said. "Thanks for taking the message. I look forward to seeing you again soon."

She gave me a warm smile. "Play some good defense for us, Mr. Cliff."

TWO

OSCAR

We came off stage bouncing with energy. The eight of us had bonded fast when we'd started rehearsals for this tour. Six weeks into the three-month tour and we were a tight group.

"Can we just stay here?" Alexi asked in his light accent. "I love how often they gasp or randomly applaud."

"Right?" Corey draped his arms around Alexi's and Matteo's shoulders. "The other audiences were wonderful, but here you can tell they are very into what we're doing."

"It vibrates the stage sometimes," I said, stopping at the door to the dressing room I shared with Nate.

"Especially for you two," Alexi continued. "They loved the pas de deux."

Nate and I traded a smile. We knew we'd scored a special dance in the show when we were learning it. I felt blessed getting to tell such an incredible story. Even in the Midwest towns we'd played so far, it had gotten a good response. Tonight, though, the loudness of the audience had thumped through me like a drumbeat at a rock concert.

"You're going to have a ton of programs to sign tonight, no doubt about it," Corey called back from his door farther down the hall.

Everyone drifted into their dressing rooms to get cleaned up and changed. The rooms here were nice—each had two stations and there was enough room not to trip over each other. We'd been to a couple of venues where we were all stuffed into a single room.

I sat at my table in front of the mirror and before I got into the routine of removing the stage makeup, a note caught my attention. The white paper almost faded into the white of the table, but the front had my name spelled out in block letters.

"No way!" I said far louder than I'd meant to as I read it.

Only one person called me O-man.

"What?" Nate looked at me through the reflections in the mirrors.

"One of my best friends growing up is here tonight." I held up the note. "I need to make sure they let him in. Be back in a sec."

Moving quickly, I went to the desk at the stage door. Hopefully, Dix wouldn't just stand outside. The last time we'd seen each other was right after third grade ended. He'd gone off to hockey camp for the summer and I'd gone to a ballet intensive. Except I never went back to

Wisconsin because my family decided to move to Miami so I could continue with that ballet school.

Over the years I'd thought about reaching out, but it'd been one of those things I'd think about and then forget. Even when he played in Miami, I never went to seek him out. I had followed his NHL career, though, and had a note in my calendar to "find Dix" while I was in New York.

The stage door opened just as I came around the corner.

Holy crap! Dixon looked good. Damn good. He was slightly taller than me, broad across the shoulders, and so handsome with close-cropped dark hair and a beard that were a few shades darker than his skin.

Our eyes locked as we stopped to stare.

"Dix!" I broke the spell, and we came together to share a backslapping embrace.

"O-man." His deep baritone voice exuded confidence and a certain sexiness too. It was far from the squeaky voices we'd had so many years ago. "You were incredible."

We stepped back and neither of us could stop grinning.

"I can't believe you're here. I'm glad you liked the show."

"Liked doesn't come close to describing how good tonight was. I can't think of another performance that moved me like your dance at the end of act one."

"Thank you. That means a lot, especially from someone who saw me wander aimlessly around the stage as a mouse in *The Nutcracker* for a couple of Christmases."

"You've come a long way." The slight laugh as he said that sent warmth through me.

"So have you, Mister Empire. I was going to look you up, but you found me first."

"Do you maybe have time tonight to grab a bite or a drink or something?"

"I'd love that." I didn't hesitate. While the cast usually had a late dinner together, we each skipped that sometimes to hang out with friends or family. "Come with me. I'll show you where you can hang out while I get changed."

"Great."

Dix officially signed in with the stage door guard, and I took the moment to look him over. The kid was still there with his bright eyes, always taking everything in. He still bubbled with enthusiasm too. He'd always been game to do whatever and I loved that that seemed unchanged.

He'd also become devastatingly handsome. I'd seen pictures online, but seeing him in hockey gear didn't compare to the dark blue suit and gray overcoat he wore, which perfectly complemented his dark brown skin. The complete package was ridiculously sexy and could've come right out of *GQ*.

I shouldn't think things like *sexy*. We were old friends and we'd only just said hi for the first time in years.

"You still into pancakes?" Dix's question pulled me out of my thoughts.

"Like you have to ask."

"Excellent. If you're up for a trip downtown, I'll take you to my favorite pancakes in the city."

He fell in next to me as I walked us farther into the backstage area.

"Is your mom okay with you eating other people's pancakes? Hers are the best. I remember the huge fundraising breakfasts your team threw. They raised a lot of cash because of her recipe."

"She still does those too, even though I grew out of that league years ago." Dix's smile radiated joy that shot right through my chest. "And she loves the pancakes at this place."

"Well, okay then. If they've got Mama Cliff's stamp of approval, I must have them." I stopped at the door to the green room. A couple of other people were already waiting for other dancers. "You can chill here. I'll be quick."

"No hurry. The place is open twenty-four seven. Plus you've got a bit of a crowd waiting for autographs and you don't want to disappoint them."

A crowd? We always signed autographs for whoever waited, but usually it was only a couple dozen people at most. "Right. Be back soon."

Dix's patience proved endless. While I'd changed quickly, there was indeed a crowd—the largest we'd seen yet—and it slowed down our departure. As we headed outside, he assured me that he understood because he always made time to talk with fans who took the time to wait.

Sometimes, as I moved from person to person, I'd look around and see him waiting in the distance, sitting on a bench and watching. Every time I looked his way I got a smile, a nod, or both.

Damn it.

My brain suddenly focused on what I was wearing—jeans, sweatshirt, leather jacket. I only dressed up for opening night at each stop and went very casual and comfortable otherwise. With Dix so dashing in his suit, I was way underdressed.

It took forty-five minutes to get to the end of the people waiting for a picture, autograph, or simply to talk about the performance. I appreciated everyone but was so happy when it was done.

"You're popular," Dix said as I stopped in front of him.

"Sorry that took so long. That's the largest crowd we've ever had. I'm guessing you get that a lot too."

He shrugged as bashfulness crossed his face. "I'm still new here, but there are fans who want to see me and I'm happy to spend time with them. You were like a rockstar here. You and your partner in that duet talked and signed so much."

"It's amazing how people react to that piece. It means different things to nearly everyone. I'm so lucky to dance it."

"Let's head to the diner so we're not talking in the

cold." Dix had the same thought I did. Even as kids, we'd had a knack for getting distracted and being late. "Subway or Lyft?"

"Which is faster?"

"On a Thursday night, probably the subway."

We walked toward the Sixty-Sixth Street subway station to catch the 1 train.

"I've never seen anything like that pas de deux." Dix talked as we navigated around the other people on the sidewalk. "I don't think I've cried as much at a performance either. No one warned me to bring Kleenex. At least I knew at *Giselle* I'd need tissues."

Pride swelled in my chest at bringing out that reaction from him.

"Even worse that it was at the end of the act and the lights came up. I'm not sure what the kid next to me thought. His mom came through with a tissue, though."

"I'm so glad that it meant something to you. I've danced a lot of powerful pieces over the years, but nothing quite like that. Rehearsals often brought me to tears, and I worried I wouldn't be able to find the right tone for the audience, or worse, that I'd get overemotional in the moment."

We headed down the stairs as our conversation continued. Since there were three other shows playing at Lincoln Center, the platform was full of audience, cast, and crew all departing.

"And you choreographed too. I noticed you did the *Swan Lake* solo yourself. It's wonderful to see how much you've accomplished." He swiped a card at the turnstile and walked through. Then he reached back to swipe for me.

"Thanks for that." I gestured at the turnstile before I followed him down the platform. "All of us got to create for the show. That scared me because I hadn't done anything for performance. It's one thing to mess around with moves in the studio and very different to create for an audience. Thank God the show's director and choreographer helped sharpen it. I learned a lot going through that process."

His gaze locked on mine and that warmth spread through me again. Without speaking, he conveyed an enormous compliment through just his eyes. I pushed myself not to look away since it filled me with pride and overwhelmed me at the same time.

"You've done so much of what you talked about when we were kids."

"So have you."

He shrugged modestly. "Still working on a Stanley Cup."

"And I'm not a principal dancer yet." I knocked into his shoulder as the train approached. "We've still got plenty of time."

"True," he shouted as the train approached.

The car we stepped into was crowded, so we stood and held on to one of the poles. We attempted to keep the conversation going, but between the screeching of the train and all the chatter around us, we settled into a comfortable silence for the ride.

THREE

DIXON

THE FORCED STOP to conversation on the subway gave me a moment to have a desperately needed reset.

Oscar had grown into an incredible-looking man. The black-and-white photo in the program didn't do him justice. His brown skin still set off his light brown eyes in a way I hadn't fully appreciated as a kid. The curls on top of his head beckoned me to touch them and to know what they felt like, which would've been wildly inappropriate.

From the performance, I knew a lot about his body since he'd danced shirtless twice—his upper body was smooth, lithe, and muscular. While he'd mostly been in tights or loose pants, he'd danced in skimpy shorts once and had shown off powerful legs. I wanted to explore it all up close.

I shouldn't have been thinking about that.

He was an old friend, not someone I should want to pick up.

But damn, it'd be a lie to say I didn't wonder what it

would be like to go down that path. My gaydar had gone on the fritz too—was he straight, bi, gay, pan, ace? I wasn't getting good clues and that might be for the best.

We got off the train at Chambers Street after what had to be the slowest trip down from Sixty-Sixth Street.

"So on that last thing you said, aren't you a principal dancer in this show?" I asked as we walked up the stairs to street level.

"I'm considered one of the *stars*." He made air quotes in front of his face. "The eight of us have equal billing, as it should be. Back home, I'm a soloist. Doing the tour probably keeps me in that position longer since I took a leave of absence to do this. I'll get there, though."

"I read in your bio that you're still in Miami. You like it there?"

"Oh man. I love it. The city has a great vibe, and it's warm."

"Did you try to find the warmest ballet company you could?" I chuckled. Oscar hated the cold. Even as a kid, it'd been nearly impossible to get him to play in the snow.

His laugh floated on the air like a soft melody. "I could've tried for the desert in Phoenix, but Miami is a great troupe. I'm glad they accepted me into their program all those years ago."

We got to the diner and I opened the door with a flourish. The place hummed with conversation.

"Dixon!" Camilla, the hostess, greeted me. "Didn't expect to see you the night before you head out."

"Had to bring an old friend in for pancakes."

"Great. We will not disappoint." She grabbed menus

from under the podium and led us through the closely spaced tables. She brought us to a two-person booth in the corner, which was my favorite since it was out of the way and also allowed for a great view of the downtown skyline.

The bell next to the cash register pinged, and she looked over. "Can't they see I'm seating someone important?" She rolled her eyes. "I'll catch up with you later." She laid the menus down. "James will take care of you." With that, she darted off to the register.

"So you come here a lot?" Oscar had a playful tone.

"Yeah," I said proudly as a busboy came and filled our water glasses. "It's my neighborhood diner. I'm probably here too much, but I can't resist the pancakes or the club sandwich."

"I've got a place near me that does insanely good Dominican food. I try to not go overboard, but I could seriously eat it for every meal."

"The hazards of having to keep fit. Although I'm glad I don't have to fit into tight costumes like you do. No one cares what I look like, so I get a little more leeway, I imagine."

"From what I see, you're looking good." Oscar's right hand flew up to his mouth as red flooded his cheeks. "Oh God. I did not just say that." His hand muffled the words.

Reaching across the table, I removed his hand, brought it back to the table, and held it. "I appreciate it. And it's okay. I've thought the same about you. You grew up great."

He held my gaze, but the red deepened.

"Thanks," he said through a very shy, very cute smile.

Electricity shot through my hand where we touched. Neither of us moved. Did he feel it too?

Discussing our looks had been awkward but also sweet. My chest had tingled when he said I looked good. I hadn't expected it or the reaction that rolled through me.

"So, uh, do you enjoy living here?" Oscar kicked our conversation back into gear. Neither of us moved our hands, though.

"It's been a lot to get used to. I went to college in Minneapolis and that wasn't much different from home. Starting my NHL career in Nashville also didn't prepare me for what it's like living in a big city like this. There's always something going on and it's always busy. I swear during the first three months, the buzz of the city exhausted me."

Oscar slid his hand out from under mine to grab his small water glass and drink it down.

"Oh yeah. Don't forget the hydration." I grinned. "You've had the workout tonight."

James arrived, luckily with a pitcher in hand. "Good evening. Dixon, good to see you as always. I hear you're introducing our pancakes to someone new." James topped off Oscar's glass.

"News travels fast."

"We've been talking too much. I haven't even looked at the menu." Oscar opened the large menu and flipped through the pages.

"I can come back." James looked between us.

Turning to Oscar, I said, "Trust me?"

"Of course. Especially with food."

I nodded and picked up my closed menu and handed it to James. "Two orders of blueberry pancakes with crispy bacon on the side. I'll take a Diet Coke with it." I looked to Oscar for his drink order.

"I'll stick with water." Oscar handed over his menu.

"Got it. I'll be back in a few minutes." James left us with a nod before stopping at the table next to us.

"So tell me everything." Oscar leaned forward. "What are the highlights of the past twenty years?"

I chuckled. "Is that all?"

"It's a start at least." He folded his hands and put them on the table in front of himself, content to wait.

"So we stayed in Madison and Mom and Dad are still there. I went to Minnesota on scholarship and majored in sports management because I'm fascinated by the business. Going into the draft, I felt so lucky having taken those classes."

James headed our way with a tray of pancakes and bacon, one of my favorite things to see.

"Get ready for some good food," I said as James arrived.

"How did that happen so fast?"

"They don't mess around."

"No, we don't, especially when there's a hungry hockey player here. So I brought extra bacon." James set a plate in the middle of the table that was almost overflowing. He looked at Oscar. "Make sure Dixon doesn't eat it all." He then put down plates of pancakes, syrup, and my soda along with a pitcher of water. "Enjoy. Let me know if you need anything."

I grabbed two pieces of bacon and chomped on them, enjoying the crispy crunch. Perfect.

Oscar shook his head and looked very amused. "I swear this could be your mother's kitchen table."

We set about getting the pancakes prepped.

Oscar finally took his first bite. I waited for his reaction as I ate my first forkful. The moan combined with the flutter of his eyes said it all.

"Oh my God. Your mom is actually back there cooking, right? These are amazing."

"That's why she approves."

I talked more and ate less so he'd be able to enjoy the food while it was hot. I covered the highlights of playing minors in Milwaukee, getting called up to Nashville, and then the trade that landed me in New York at the start of the season.

"That's a lot of moving in five years." He dragged a slice of bacon through the syrup on his plate.

"Yeah. Luckily, I keep things pretty lean, so moving is easy."

"I've moved three times in twenty years. We spent the first year in an apartment until Mom and Dad found a house they liked. They're still in that house and then I moved into my own place when I turned twenty-one." He took more bacon and repeated the action with the syrup.

I stared as he ate the bacon and then licked his fingers.

I wanted to do that for him... or maybe that would be *to him*.

"What about family? Married? Kids?"

Those questions coming right after wanting to lick him gave me pause. "Not yet. Haven't found a forever guy yet." I decided to put it out there. No need to skirt around the question of husband or wife.

"Me either. I haven't dated much since getting my heart smashed a few years ago."

Oscar was looking for a guy too? Or was he speaking in broad terms?

Maybe I could lick him.

Shit.

I couldn't think like that, especially after hearing it was a bad break up.

I managed not to visibly shake my head to clear it and get it off that track. Hopefully, Oscar couldn't pick up on how many things were colliding in my brain.

"It is so good to see you," Oscar said. "I wished I'd connected sooner. Time just gets away, you know?"

I chewed as I nodded in acknowledgement. "I imagine we're similar. Practice, practice, practice and then it's play the game or do the performance, and the cycle repeats. When you're not doing that, you're recovering and catching up on the most immediate things going on. At least that's how it feels for me."

"I swear if my family didn't make sure I put Sunday dinner on the calendar, I wouldn't make it. I get caught up in doing what I love, so I really can't complain either."

"Even with all the time gone, I'm glad we're able to fall back into talking so easily."

"Right? This could've been all kinds of awkward." He paused again for a drink. "Tell me, what are you doing this week? I've got free time during the day. I'd love to get together more, maybe watch you practice if that's allowed. I imagine your games happen at the same time I'm on stage."

I sighed. Excitement vibrated through me that he wanted to hang more. If only I could call in sick. "I leave town in the morning for six days. Headed for a string of games on the West Coast."

"Well damn. Talk about terrible timing." Oscar didn't mask his disappointment.

I awkwardly reached into my pants pocket and pulled out my phone, which got me a raised eyebrow from Oscar. That was cuter than it had any right to be.

"Give me your number. I don't want to lose touch." I unlocked my phone and handed it to him.

He took it and typed on the screen, then held it out and snapped a selfie. He knew how to pose for the camera, angling his head just so and with the sweetest of smiles. But did he know how much his eyes smoldered? Did he always do that or was it just for that shot?

His phone vibrated from somewhere. "There. Now I've got you too."

He handed my phone back as, in a smoother move than I'd managed, he got his out. He swiped, tapped, and pointed the camera at me. I smirked as he snapped.

"Oh my God. You still can't take a serious picture."

"You do not know how much PR people hate me when they do headshots."

We talked way longer than we should've. I loved every minute and fully realized how much I'd missed having Oscar in my life. We used to see each other every day, but when he'd moved, that had been it. It'd happened way before I had my own phone or social media.

Now we had no excuse to lose touch. Hopefully, Oscar's texting game was as strong as mine.

"You're extra super happy," Nate said when I walked into our dressing room. "Are you humming?" He turned to watch me as I set my Starbucks down and slipped out of my coat. Meanwhile, I couldn't get "Miss You Much" out of my head. Dix's mom loved Janet Jackson and her music had played in their house a lot, especially the *Rhythm Nation* album.

"What's got you in the Ms. Jackson mood this morning?"

I caught my goofy grin in the mirror behind Nate.

"Does this have anything to do with the guy you left with last night?"

Even though I wanted to be curled up asleep since I hadn't gotten back to the hotel until near two, the happiness of seeing Dix had powered me to be back at the theater at ten. The cast often did educational events, and today we were meeting with students from the School of American Ballet to talk about our experiences in the profession and on this tour. Thankfully, after that I could nap before tonight's show.

My mind churned most of the night on what it would've been like to go home with Dix. It turned out he lived across the street from the diner. He'd been so sweet too, offering to ride with me back to the hotel. I'd told him to go get some sleep since he'd had the early flight, but he'd waited with me until the car showed up. When we hugged goodbye, I'd really wanted to kiss him but I just didn't have the nerve. Kissing him, however, had woven its way into my dreams. In those dreams, he was a fantastic kisser.

"Spill. You said he was someone you hadn't seen in years."

I covered my face with my hand, knowing I'd blush soon if I wasn't already. "Wouldn't you rather just dance to Janet before we meet the kids?"

I continued humming, louder this time, and doing some *Rhythm Nation* choreography, hoping to distract him.

He jumped up, stood next to me, and perfectly matched my moves. The album had come out a good decade before either of us was born, but it was a classic.

"You know," he said as we grooved, "I can do this and talk at the same time, so this isn't going to keep me from asking questions."

I caught his smirk in the mirror.

"Okay. Fine." I stopped my Janet moves.

Truth was that Nate usually roomed with me, but we were in his home city, so he was spending time with his husband. Since I was actually eager to talk to someone about Dix, I dropped onto the couch that was on the side of the room opposite the makeup tables. Nate spun his chair around so he could sit on it backward.

"So, yeah, Dix and I grew up in the same neighborhood, played together, went to school together. We were probably as tight as two nine-year-olds could be."

"The oldest friend I have is from high school. I barely remember the names of anyone before that."

I fiddled with the silver ring I wore on my right middle finger. It'd been a gift from my parents when I joined the Miami City Ballet. They'd said it was to be a reminder that they believed in me. It'd become a touchstone for me anytime I was unsure.

"We lived two houses apart, and we were always together. The other kids on the street who were our age didn't have the practices we did—I was already in ballet class and he had hockey. We looked out for each other too. Not everyone understood the boy who wanted to dance but Dix did."

Nate nodded. "It's cool you've reconnected."

"I was so mad when we moved. I didn't get to say goodbye, but writing letters never crossed my mind at that age. Plus I got caught up in school and all that stuff. Yet there were plenty of times I'd want to see and talk to my friend." I took a sip from my cooling coffee.

Nate looked thoughtful. "I played soccer when I was that age, but I don't remember having a friendship like that. On the street I grew up, there were people I hung out with because they were there, but I'm pretty sure if anyone showed up here and said hello I wouldn't remember them."

"He's the only one I remember from back then. I thought about this when I got back last night. He was always nice. When others laughed at or ignored someone, he always wanted to be a friend or to help. No one was left on the sideline when Dix was around. He was also game to do anything, and that somehow meant I'd do anything he wanted to."

"Anything?"

"Not only would he make his parents get him to any performance I had, he'd build Legos with me all day long, even on nice days when he'd rather be outside. But I'd also go outside and do what he wanted sometimes and I'd even go skating with him, even though I hated the cold. I'd say it was pretty balanced. Oh, and we were also kick ass at school projects. We both loved making a good diorama with our parents."

"OMG. How do you remember all that? I mostly remember TV that I watched at that age."

"I guess he left an impression."

"I'd say." Nate leaned forward and lowered his voice. "Was he always so good-looking?"

"Hey now, what would Todd say if he heard that?" I couldn't resist picking on Nate a little.

"He'd ask to see pictures. We guy watch all the time." He raised his eyebrows a couple of times.

"A perk of being together for a few years, I suppose."

"Among the many, yes."

The intercom above the door crackled to life.

"Dancers to the stage, please. The students are on the way."

We stood, and I drank down the coffee since I didn't want to take the cup to the stage.

"And to answer your question, Dix grew up hot. That's for sure. Sitting across from him last night..."

"Oh? Go on."

Nate and I had become fast, tight friends during rehearsals, which was great since we danced the duet. Even this more personal thing seemed okay to talk about with him.

"Some looks we shared. Moments we stopped talking but kept staring at each other. The jolts I got if we touched. Not to mention some of the things that came out of my mouth." I stopped short of telling him my most embarrassing moment when I'd essentially told Dix he was hot.

"Any idea if he felt the same?"

We walked on stage as students assembled in the audience seats. Corey and Alexi already sat on stools at the front of the stage. I heard others coming up behind us.

"Maybe." I kept my voice low. "Not sure if it was just me projecting."

"Can you see him again? Find out if there's a spark. You totally should. What a story that would be to find each other out of the blue twenty years later and fall for each other."

"Whoa, whoa, whoa. That's a lot too fast, don't you think?" Since the students were still arriving, I stopped and let the four dancers behind us pass to lessen the chance I'd get overheard. I liked these guys, but they didn't need to know everything. "Besides, he left today to play for a week on the West Coast." Disappointment permeated my response.

"Damn."

"Exactly."

Did I even want to know if we had a spark? We lived on opposite ends of the East Coast, so anything beyond a friendship seemed impossible. But even last night there'd been a feeling in my heart that I'd never had with anyone else.

Nate put his arm around my shoulders. "Sorry, man. For what it's worth, Todd and I were only together a couple of months before I went out on the *America's Next Top Dancer* tour. Five years later and we're still going strong, even as I travel a good bit out of every year."

I nodded as we took our places as the last of the students got seated and our director, Calvin, came up to the stage with someone I guessed was one of the teachers.

There'd be plenty of time to mull my feelings over. In the meantime, the discussion with the students provided a perfect distraction.

FIVE

DIXON

Exhaustion fogged my brain as I arrived at the airport. Not only had I stayed out too late, but thoughts of Oscar had kept me awake even after I'd lain down. There'd been lots of thinking about the possible flirting we'd done.

I couldn't decide if it'd been real or if it'd been all in my head. I'd also spent too much time regretting my decision not to kiss him. He'd been right there. I could've taken the chance. What was there to lose? If he'd kissed me back, that would've been amazing. If he'd told me it wasn't what he wanted, I'd have been embarrassed, but we could also go back to not seeing each other pretty easily.

If that kiss had been good, though—and I knew in my heart it would've been—what would that have meant? It wasn't like we'd be able to immediately hang out again. By the time I was back, he'd be off somewhere else.

Reconnecting had been awesome. The zings from

touching him and the couple of smoldering gazes he'd sent my way ran in a constant loop in my head and added to the regret of not going for the kiss. After all, if I'd done that, it'd also be on replay instead of just an imagined version of it.

He was so damn cute and handsome. Being with him was so comfortable too. I'd been a little worried that we'd sit down and not have much to talk about, but the conversation had flowed easily. When we were kids, we could go from being chatterboxes—as my mother called it—while we played video games to hanging out quietly and reading. We seemed to still have that, given how our time at the diner had gone.

Moving Oscar from the friend zone to something more seemed nearly impossible and completely impractical. How would a New York-Miami relationship work? Could we ever be more than friends?

"You okay?" Team captain Caleb Carter put his arm around my shoulders as I joined him and our other teammates hanging around the terminal waiting to board. "You look rough. Not getting sick, are you?" As soon as he asked, he stepped back, as did a couple of the other guys.

"Nah, man. Just tired." I dropped my backpack to the floor and braced it between my feet. "Ended up staying out too late last night."

"Did you finally get a hookup?" Dimitri asked. It was common knowledge that it'd been a while since I'd had any sort of date, and Dimitri was a cheerleader for making sure everyone had enough sex.

I wished I had.

Or did I really?

If we'd kissed, would we have taken it up to my place to go further? A hookup with Oscar would've been hot but also probably the worst idea. It would've been way too fast. Although I thought of what it might be like to hold him close, to find out what he liked done to him and what he might want to do to me.

It didn't do me any good to think about that now, but my mind didn't want to get that message. The fantasy and reality blurred together where my imagination was concerned.

I shook my head, and Dimitri rolled his eyes. I hadn't even been here a full season and the team and I already knew so much about each other. They'd been an easy group to become part of because they'd been so welcoming.

"Just met up with someone I hadn't seen in years and we spent more time catching up than we should've."

The door opened to the tarmac, and everyone grabbed their carry-ons. I slung my pack onto one shoulder and moved alongside Caleb.

"Didn't you go to a show last night?"

"Yeah. And talk about a small world. One dancer was someone who'd lived down the street from me in Madison."

He shook his head with a look of surprise on his face. "It's so cool when that happens. I remember in college lining up for a face-off across from someone I'd met in hockey camp. We'd gotten into position and then recognized each other. The ref didn't know what to make of our 'Hey man, how's it going?' thing, as if we'd forgotten we were in the middle of an important game."

"That sounds very Cole and Miles," I said, thinking about one of our centers and his best friend, and now boyfriend, who plays for Detroit.

"Right. I flashback to the moment sometimes when I watch them have a conversation over the face-off dot."

As we boarded, I told him about our time at the diner. "Can I ask you…" I trailed off. I wasn't sure if my question might cross a line but I continued since he was giving me an expectant look. "How soon did you know you wanted more with Aaron when you two reconnected?"

Ugh. That sounded terrible.

"Sorry." I backpedaled fast. "You don't have to answer that."

He got the look that he often did with younger players—the one that said not to worry about whatever stupid thing they'd just done. I didn't know much about Caleb and Aaron's story other than it'd happened while he was recuperating from an injury.

Dimitri took his usual seat but instead of sitting next to him, Caleb gestured for me to go into the row across. I tossed my bag in the overhead and sat as he did the same. Dimitri looked confused for a moment since Caleb always sat with him, but he popped his AirPods in and leaned back.

"It was pretty immediate. The crush I had on him from high school roared back at first sight. That's not to say it was easy from there, but it turned out we'd had crushes on each other, so it gave us something to build on."

That was an easy one.

"I don't think we had crushes at eight and nine." The mere thought of that amused me since we'd been far more into Legos, video games, riding bikes, and practicing our respective passions. "If we lived in the same city or even the same state, I'd want to ask him out."

"Do it anyway." I couldn't tell if that was more a statement or a question. Was he trying to talk me into it?

"Florida seems like next-level long distance."

"But we're in Miami a few times a season and there's quite a few months in the off season."

"You think I should?" I wasn't sure if I wanted him to encourage me or not.

"I don't like what-ifs. If you think there's something worth going for, do it. Do you know if he's even open to it? Having a conversation isn't bad. I'm a big believer in talking."

The flight attendant announced the door was closing and that we'd take off soon.

"We promised to stay in touch. Is it weird having that kind of conversation on the phone or through texts?" So many thoughts fought for space. I wasn't even looking for a relationship, but suddenly I wanted this even though it seemed impossible to get.

"Sometimes it's the only way to do it. Neither of you can take a spur-of-the-moment vacation."

I nodded. "You're right about the what-ifs. I'm fixated

on *what if he's the one*. I've never asked myself that question before, even with someone I've dated."

Caleb smiled. "There you go. I'm guessing he hasn't said anything to make you think he's not open to it."

"Nothing I can think of. We managed to confirm that we're not straight, so I guess there's not much to lose."

Caleb raised his eyebrows. "The worst that happens is you get a no. But if the best happens... think how great that will be. I can't imagine a life without Aaron in it now."

I ran my hand across my beard and then over my head. He spoke truth.

"I'll think about all that while I try to get a nap."

"Sleep thinks are the best." He put his fist out and I bumped it. "I'll leave you to it. Plus if I don't go over there, Dimitri's going to get all superstitious about this trip."

We laughed as he got up and took his seat across the aisle. I definitely didn't want to cause Dimitri to get fixated on where Caleb was sitting. I had my travel routine, which consisted of listening to the same playlist at takeoff. The one time I hadn't listened to it, we'd had an aborted takeoff that was one of the scariest moments I'd ever had while traveling.

If I asked and Oscar didn't want to try a relationship, maybe we'd just get a good laugh out of it.

I fiddled with my phone to start the music and put in my AirPods. I dozed off before the safety announcements, with John Legend in my ears and thoughts of Oscar bouncing around in my head.

SIX

MESSAGES FROM THE ROAD

Dixon: Hi from somewhere over the middle of the country.

Oscar: Hey. Nothing better than wi-fi on the plane to pass the time.

Dixon: Totally.

Oscar: Surprised you're not sleeping after our late night.

Dixon: Woke up for lunch and wanted to say hello. How's your day going?

Oscar: Up way too early to talk to some students. I forgot about that until the alarm went off. Thank goodness I usually preset alarms so I don't have to think about it right before sleep.

Dixon: Ouch. Sorry you had an early morning.

Oscar: Pfff. Totally worth it. I had a great time with you. You sort of came up during our Q&A with students this morning. One student asked me what I thought of touring. I started with the practical that it was interesting to watch the machinery that makes a tour work, but that it's very different than being in your home theater every night. One of the great parts is seeing places you might not get to on your own. Sometimes you also get to reconnect with someone you hadn't seen in a while.

Dixon: Being in so many different arenas and hotels so often took time for me to get used to when I started playing in the minors. The travel was more limited before that. The weird thing now, after playing in the league for so long, is that I just keep going back to the same places— even the hotels in the cities are usually the same.

Oscar: Maybe you should come talk to these students too. You're on the road much more than I am.

Dixon: LOL! Do you travel much with Miami?

Oscar: Sometimes, usually in state or in the Southeast. I wouldn't mind more travel, maybe an actual vacation instead of work.

Dixon: Where would you want to go?

Oscar: My bucket list for travel is to do a tour around the world to see ballet companies. The Royal, the Bolshoi, Paris Opera Ballet, I've got a list of twenty that are split pretty evenly between the US and internationally. Beyond that big one, I'd like to go where there's a good beach and even better food.

Dixon: That trip sounds amazing, and so does the beach, but in a different way.

Oscar: In what way?

Dixon: So the beach is different just because it's so relaxing. The ballet trip needs planning and minding a schedule. I love vacations where there's a minimal plan or even no set plan.

Oscar: I'm with you on that. I love having no plan when possible. Don't get me wrong, I like a good schedule but sometimes you shouldn't have to keep one too.

Dixon: Yes! Absolutely. So, would you maybe like some company for those trips?

Oscar: If it's you, then yes. I've been working on saving up the money for the ballet trip. But I bet we can find a beach to go to pretty easily.

Dixon: I know we could.

Oscar: Oh, you know, I should've looked. Do you play tonight after the flight?

Dixon: No. Thank God. Dinner and sleep once we're in Anaheim. Light skate tomorrow morning and then afternoon game. We'll take a charter bus after to LA to be there for Sunday night.

Oscar: I'm glad we're playing a week at a time in each city. I don't think I'd like moving every day or two.

Dixon: It takes some getting used to for sure. The league makes it about as easy as it can be, though. If you ever want to see a hardcore schedule, I should show you the details we get for trips like this when we're out for so long. I'm thankful for it because it tells me all I need to know.

Oscar: The tour logistic people are great too. The overall schedule, plus details on each city, and every night we get a reminder about what we need to do the next day.

Dixon: Speaking of your tour. I just checked your schedule and I'm glad I did. We've got overlap in Denver next week, and then Dallas the week after.

Oscar: !

Dixon: Is that good or bad?

Oscar: It's everything good! We get to hang out?

Dixon: I'd love that.

Oscar: ...

Dixon: Those three dots just keep going. Are you writing a book?

Oscar: Sorry.

Dixon: Aww. Don't do that. Tell me what you wanted to say. It's cool.

Oscar: Well. I didn't want to seem overexcited.

Dixon: I get it... neither did I. Fact is, I want to see you. Last night was great to catch up, but I didn't want to go home.

Oscar: Glad I wasn't the only one.

Dixon: Good. Saves me being embarrassed.

Oscar: Ha! Can the big hockey player be embarrassed?

Dixon: Just as easily as when I was a kid.

Oscar: OMG! I remember how upset you got when you

slipped and fell on your ass coming in from recess in first grade. Wet boots on wet tile and you went down. The kids were merciless about how you could skate but couldn't manage to walk.

Dixon: I've tried to bury that. They only teased me more as they saw how angry I got. What I always remember is you pushing through them to offer me a hand up from the floor.

Oscar: You helped me all the time. No way I could just leave you there.

Dixon: We always were a good team.

Oscar: Right! Remember how good we were in capture the flag.

Dixon: We had an excellent strategy. At least until everyone figured out that we shouldn't play together. Maybe we should've become spies like we talked about.

Oscar: How do you know I'm not?

Dixon: LOL

Oscar: I hate I have to do this, but I've got to go. The show's publicist is here to get me to an interview on one of the afternoon news shows. Text me or, even better, call me later?

Dixon: I'll do that. If I don't talk to you before, have a good show tonight.

Oscar: Thanks! Later.

SEVEN

OSCAR

"Oh, come on, ref!"

I took a deep breath to center myself and leaned over until my chest was flat against my legs. I stayed down as the commentators dissected a replay that apparently clearly showed the refs were wrong and should've called for goalie interference.

A few days ago, I'd watched a bunch of YouTube videos on hockey rules so I'd be able to appreciate the sport more when I watched Dix. When we were kids, all I'd cared about was the goals. Now, though, I enjoyed knowing the actual rules. It was pretty simple, really, outside of the nuances of the penalties, which relied on the refs. In this case, the ref was crap.

"I never imagined we'd be watching hockey while we warmed up," Nate said as he dropped to the floor next to me and started his stretches.

I rolled my torso up slowly as Nate spread his legs out

to stretch while working on his arms. We both wore loose T-shirts and shorts.

"Sorry." I turned the sound down.

"No. No. Really, it's fine. It's on at home sometimes since Todd's a New York fan. I think he's hoping you and Dixon become a thing so that maybe he can score some good tickets from you."

I moved my legs so the bottoms of my feet touched and my legs were out to the sides. "So that's how it is, is it?" I looked over and raised an eyebrow.

"In the time we've lived in New York, Todd and I have made a lot of connections, but none that we know of have anything to do with hockey. I know Todd would get Dixon anything he wanted for Lincoln Center."

Nate had been a great listener since Dixon and I had started talking and texting a few times a day. I tried not to bore him, but I could only roll over the same questions in my head so many times before I had to talk to someone else about what I was thinking.

"I'm actually glad that someone else is invested in this if we try to move things to the next level."

"Well"—Nate bent forward until his chest was touching his legs like I'd done earlier—"the choice is one hundred percent yours, but Todd and I are in favor of you at least giving it a shot."

I stood and raised my leg onto the barre that ran along our dressing room wall. "I'm excited I get to see him for a few hours next week."

He brought himself back into a sitting position. "Have you thought about what you're going to do?"

"Probably just hang out at the hotel since time is short, unless we—" On the screen, the game had stopped and the focus was on a New York player laid out on the ice. He was on his side and across his back the letters *CLI* were visible along with the number four.

"Oscar?" Nate looked from me to where the phone sat on the floor, propped against a book.

"Oh shit." Nate grabbed the phone and turned up the sound.

I scrambled over and sat next to Nate on the floor.

"...we'll be back after a few messages."

"How can they just go to commercial like that?"

Before the ad started, someone with a medical bag had just gotten to Dix, who had rolled onto his back by himself. His teammates stood over him, with the other team standing back. How had that even happened? I'd missed whatever put him on the ice.

A knot of anxiety formed in my stomach, worse than any stage fright I'd ever had. I took a deep breath, held it for five seconds, and then slowly released it. I couldn't allow this to affect tonight's performance.

"I'm sure he's okay. He's got all that padding, right?"

"I guess." But I was far from sure. This was the second game I'd watched in the last few days, and in the first one there hadn't been any injuries that had required the trainer to go out on the ice. Would it always be nail-biting to watch a friend play? How did his parents handle it?

"And we're back. The face-off is in the neutral zone. We'll have an update on Dixon Cliff at intermission. He skated off the ice with a member of the training staff, although he was favoring his left leg. And the puck—"

"Good evening, amazing dancers," Pamela, our stage manager, announced over the PA, "it's seven o'clock and this is your half-hour call."

I reached over, took the phone from Nate, and turned it off. "At least they didn't have to carry him off."

I typed out a message to him.

Oscar: Hope you're okay! Nate and I were watching during our warm-ups. We're sending you lots of healing vibes.

Nate laid his arm around my shoulders and drew me into a hug. "He'll be fine. They've got excellent doctors just like we do."

"I know." I leaned my head against him. "Or at least my brain knows that. It's scary to see someone down like that. I'm glad he was at least able to skate off."

"You're shaking." Nate held me a little tighter.

"Am I?" When had that started? "Sorry." I was also turning my ring back and forth, which I hadn't realized either.

"No need to apologize." Nate's concerned smile settled me a bit.

I wished there was a way to get news—anything to let me know he was really okay and something hadn't gone wrong. I'd seen too many medical shows where someone seemed mostly fine and then they weren't.

"We should go run through our lifts." I tried to say it

like I meant it when what I really wanted was to turn the game back on and see if there was news.

"You sure? We could hang for a couple more minutes."

I knew we should get going. We always held our lift work until the half hour call so it was fresh. We were already a few minutes off schedule and I didn't like to be off track.

"Yeah." I lifted my head, and he dropped his arm from around me. "Let's do this."

I stood and offered Nate a hand up.

Suddenly, he gave me a tight hug. "It'll be okay."

I nodded as he pulled back. He gestured with his head toward the door and I nodded again.

The anxiety swirling in me was unlike any I'd had before. There were preshow jitters, which I was used to and were a sign that things were good. The few times I didn't get jitters, something was off. Stress at starting something new was also common, and that was a good thing too because it usually meant I was doing the right thing by pushing myself to go beyond what I'd done before. Going into new situations and meeting new people often brought some low-level angst as well.

I thought I was aware of most of the anxiety types I could get. This one was different, and it was tight—like a guitar string stretched too far during tuning.

We walked quietly out onto the stage. Despite the curtain being down, we could still hear the murmurs of the audience entering. The sounds soothed me as the part of my brain that knew there was a job to do took over. We stood in our places, took a moment to lock eyes with each other, and nodded.

Moving at about half speed, we walked through the motions of the dance, and at each point there was a lift we did it. This was a ritual we did each night to connect. Shows that had fighting scenes did fight choreography before each show, and we did this. It was a good part of our final stretching routine but also provided a moment to focus on each other to help us be ready for our performance later.

Once we'd moved through the complex choreography, we stood, placed our hands on each other's shoulders, looked directly at each other, and counted to sixty. Nate nodded and raised his eyebrows at me and I smiled back. A couple of other dancers were on the stage now as well, quietly going through their preshow routines.

"Can I tell you something?" I glanced at Nate as we went back to our dressing room.

"Of course."

"I want more with Dix. I can't pretend that I don't. I've told myself all kinds of things about why it wouldn't work, but I want it. All the feelings balled up right here" —needing more emphasis, I waved my hand over my heart and stomach—"and that I desperately want to get on a plane to New York to check on him tells me that."

"It's almost time, dancers. This is your ten-minute call."

Despite my stress, Nate and I were back on time. In the dressing room, we each went to our racks, got our first costume, and changed. It'd felt good to say that to Nate. I needed to say it to Dix, but at the moment just saying it out loud to another person was good.

"It's next week you get to see him, right?"

"Yeah. I mean, unless he's hurt bad enough that he won't make the trip."

Nate shook his head. "Don't think like that."

"Right, right." I put on the tight, sleeveless T-shirt I wore for the first number. "He'll be there. And then I need to tell him how I feel."

I stripped off my loose warm-up shorts and got into the special jeans. They looked like denim but were stretchy Lycra, which was necessary for the dance.

Dressed and ready, I went back to my makeup table to make sure I looked good. With a couple pokes to my hair, I proclaimed myself done. Picking up my phone, I found no messages on the lock screen. Going to the app, I confirmed that what I'd sent hadn't been read yet.

That meant nothing. Dix had more important things to do than check his phone.

I sent a new message.

Oscar: Show's about to begin here. Send me a message when you can and let me know how you're doing. Sending you all the good vibes from Chicago.

"Any news?"

"No." I put the phone down and took off my ring, but not until I'd spun it around a few times. "Do I look okay?" Nate and I asked this of each other every night as part of our routine. I spun around slowly.

"Perfect. How about me?" Nate turned.

"One second." I put my hand out to stop him while his back was to me. I brushed a piece of string off his shoulder. "There. Now you're all good."

The phone screen lit up, and I grabbed it. The message was from Dix's phone, but it started with *Hi Oscar, it's Caleb...* and that was all I could see.

"It's that time, dancers. We're at five minutes and places, please."

"It's news," I said as I swiped the screen and looked at it so it'd recognize me.

Dixon: Hi Oscar, it's Caleb Carter. I'm Dixon's captain and we're in intermission here. I just got him to unlock the phone so I could text you while they work on him. He says to tell you he's okay, just annoyed they aren't letting him back on the ice tonight. Which, by the way, is normal for this kind of thing. He hopes you have a good show and says not to worry.

"That's good news," Nate said after I read it to him.

"Yeah. It is." I couldn't suppress a grin.

I texted back quickly.

Oscar: Thanks, Caleb! Dix, I'll call you after the show.

"Let's go." Nate clapped me on the back as I placed the phone on my charger.

We headed for the stage, ready to go.

EIGHT

DIXON

The next couple of days were going to be terrible.

I hadn't been hit that hard in a long time. I was a big guy, so it took a lot to knock me down, but it was one of those hits that happened in just the right way. In addition to the hit from another big guy, I also slammed into the ice.

Even with an ice bath tonight, I imagined everything would hurt tomorrow. The question was how much could I mitigate the pain I'd feel on the second day—the second day was almost always worse than the first.

At least I cleared the concussion protocol. A sharp pain in my knee was why I hadn't gotten up quickly. I didn't like to take chances, so having Nicky come out to check me had been the right call.

Since we were in the back half of the season, it was important to stay as healthy and injury free as possible. Playing with a tweaked knee could make it worse, which might mean more extended time off the ice. I never wanted that. But since I was in my first season here, all I wanted to do was show my worth by bringing my best.

So far, the consensus was that the knee was only slightly sprained. Luckily, we didn't have a game tomorrow, which meant I could work with the trainers.

Tonight's instructions were simple: ice it a couple of times and take ibuprofen before bed and again when I woke up. The only twinge I'd felt in my knee since leaving the arena was when I got into my car. Once I was home, the first thing I did was texted Oscar to let him know I'd made it.

Next it was about getting comfortable. I put on sweats, made an ice bag, and dropped onto my couch. Putting my leg up, I placed the bag so it was resting on my knee.

The phone rang, but it wasn't the ringtone I'd assigned to Oscar, which was what I'd been expecting. The display said the call was coming from the diner.

"Hello?"

"Dixon. Hi. It's Camilla. We've got a delivery for you and wanted to make sure you're home before we sent it over."

What? I hadn't ordered anything.

Maybe I had a concussion after all and was forgetting things.

"Um. Sorry. I'm afraid I didn't make an order."

"You didn't." She sounded like she was excited that she had something to share. "Your friend did, though."

The only person it could be was Oscar. I had good friends, but I couldn't imagine any of them deciding to send food from the diner over. Oscar and I had always delivered things to each other when we were sick—usually toys or books, but sometimes food our parents would make.

"Oh wow. Okay. I'm home, so you can send it over whenever."

"I'll send Marco with it now. You feel better soon."

"No better medicine than your food. Thanks so much."

"You're welcome. See you soon, Dixon. Good night."

"Good night."

Once I ended that call, I made another down to the doorman.

"Good evening, Mr. Cliff. How can I help you?"

"Hi, Toby. I've got a food delivery coming from across the street. Can you please let Marco come on up?"

"Of course. Anything else?"

"No thanks, Toby. Have a good night."

"Thanks, Mr. Cliff. You too."

Amazing. I couldn't believe he'd done that, especially since it wasn't like he didn't have his own show tonight. His text message had been a touching thought. I hadn't imagined he'd have the game on while he was getting ready, and yet it was kind of cool that he would be that interested.

Based on the time, Oscar should be doing the stage door thing. So far while he'd been in Chicago, I'd heard from him around midnight. The call should come anytime now.

I carefully got up and went to the kitchen. Once I'd

put the ice bag back in the freezer, I got a mug from the cupboard, filled it with water, and popped it in the microwave. Hot chocolate was the perfect drink.

There were three knocks on the door and I went to answer. Marco, who I knew well from my frequent deliveries, was there with a plastic bag.

"Hi. Here's your order, Dixon. Sorry to hear about what happened at the game."

"It's okay. I should be ready for the next game. Thanks for this." I held up the bag. "Oh, let me go get my wallet. Come in for a second."

"No need. It was all taken care of."

"Are you sure?" I raised a questioning eyebrow at him.

"Yes. Absolutely. Enjoy the food."

"Thank you. Have a good night."

He waved as he made his way down the hall and back to the elevators.

The smell of bacon hit me, triggering a loud stomach rumble.

In the kitchen, I took two large containers out of the bag—one with pancakes and the other with bacon. There was also a small container of syrup.

In short order, I had the pancakes and bacon in front of me ready to eat, along with a cup of cocoa. I wasted no time digging in.

Oscar was truly amazing. He'd taken care of me tonight like no one else except my parents. It was a simple gesture of food, but it was way beyond anything he'd had to do. How could I have him in my life more?

Caleb made it seem possible to do long distance, and there were many long-distance couples in the league. Sometimes people got traded, and it didn't make sense to move the entire family. They made it work.

My phone screen lit up with a FaceTime call, and Oscar's face from the selfie he took popped into view. I moved to swipe to answer but stopped short.

"Well, crap."

My fingers were covered in syrup because I wasn't eating neatly.

I grabbed some napkins and tried to clean up, but of course, the napkin stuck to me instead.

"Hang on," I said to no one.

I thought about licking my fingers, but then I'd have paper in my mouth. Times like these made me wish I'd set my phone up so I could just tell it to answer the call.

Looking at my fingers, I picked the one that looked the cleanest and tapped to take the call.

"O-man! Hi."

"Dix! It's good to hear your voice." He paused. "Um. Why am I looking at the ceiling?"

"Because I've got syrup on my hands."

Oscar's soft chuckle came across the speaker. "Oops."

"One second, let me wash this off." I went to the sink and talked loudly enough to be heard over the water. "Thanks so much for the food. I didn't realize how hungry I was until it was here. The smell of the bacon brought out the beast."

"Oh good. I'm glad you liked it. I wasn't sure how you felt about surprises, but I decided to go for it."

"I'm always down for a good surprise. That's not changed since I was a kid."

I grabbed a glass and a plate and brought them to the counter so I could stand up the phone.

"That's better," Oscar said as I sat down. "It's much better to look at you."

He looked good as usual, with a glow that I'd come to recognize from him postshow. What glow would he have after a blow job or some other fantastic sexual experience?

That was something to think about more later!

"What about you? You liked surprises even more than I did. That still true?"

"For the most part, yes."

I furrowed my brow. "Who gave you a bad surprise? I need their name. Seriously, though, what does that mean? I want to make sure I don't give a bad one."

Oscar chuckled. I hoped that meant I wasn't asking about something painful.

"I don't like surprises that involve going somewhere. I like to know where I'm going and make sure I've brought the right things with me. Even if it's just a night out, I still want to know. Now, if you're giving me something, give away! It's always fun to get something."

"Good to know. I can work with that."

"You should keep eating while we talk. Don't let that get cold."

I grabbed a piece of bacon and gestured at the screen before popping it in my mouth.

"There have been people who don't get the anxiety

that surfaces when I don't know the plan and where we're going. Sometimes they're sure I'll love it, and it only makes it worse."

Who would do that to him? Whoever it had been, they were terrible people. "I respect that. I'd never want to do something that made you feel uncomfortable."

"I doubt you could. In fact, if anyone was going to take me somewhere for a surprise, I imagine I'd be okay with you."

That was high praise that I made him feel safe like that. "I will not put you through that to find out. I'll always share the plan."

"So, how are you doing?" Oscar said, changing the subject. "What even happened? I didn't see the hit when I was stretching, just you on the ice and then a commercial."

"I'm okay. No concussion, which is good. My knee hurt a lot immediately after, which is why I didn't move right away. It's some level of sprain. I'll go in tomorrow and they'll figure out what it means. It's not very swollen, which is good. I hope, since there's no game tomorrow, that I'll be good to play the next one. We'll see."

"You'll do what they tell you, right?" There was an edge of authority to Oscar's voice.

"Oh yeah. Always. The one time I didn't follow instructions in high school, I ended up out for six weeks and hated it."

"Good. I've seen too many dancers try to push beyond what the doctors say, and it never works out."

I grunted and nodded as I finished a bite of pancakes.

"The only upside to being injured would be that I could maybe steal away to come see you."

Oscar's eyes widened and he smiled. "I don't know if I should actually hope for that or not. Seems like it would be some nasty karma if I wished for that."

"Is it bad for me to wish for that? I'm okay doing all the wishing, and that'll keep you in the clear."

Oscar's thinking face was so cute, especially since he exaggerated it, putting his fingers to his chin and looking upward. He looked like an emoji. "I don't think you want to mess with karma. Maybe just hope, like I will, that you get better as soon as you can."

I gave a sharp nod. "Yes, sir. I'm going to follow that advice."

Another laugh from him made my heart happy.

"So, how are you tonight? Good show?"

"I'm great. I enjoyed the slow day more than I expected to. So often there's promo to do during the day, and today there wasn't. I read for a while and then went with Nate to visit a friend of his who's a dancer with The Joffrey. We even joined a class there."

"You taught a class or you took a class?"

"Took. It was fun to learn from someone new and experience how they teach, what they teach. Do you ever skate for pure enjoyment?"

I thought as I drank some of my now tepid cocoa. "Not a lot."

"We may need to do that sometime if you're game. I find dancing for fun—whether it's taking a class that's different or just cutting loose in my living room—keeps me in good spirits."

I'd never considered that there could be a benefit to just skating. I'd been into that even in college, just going to skate and enjoying whatever music was playing. I hadn't done that in years.

"Yes, let's do that. I would love to skate with you."

A yawn escaped him, a sign he was coming down from the performance.

"Alright, that means it's time for bed for you."

"Yeah, sorry. It just washed over me. You should probably get some sleep too. Rest up your battered body."

"I feel a yawn coming too. I'm tired and I'm getting full."

"I'll say good night then. I'm glad you're okay."

"Thanks again for the food. And for the chat. I love ending the day with you."

We smiled

"Text me when you wake up and let me know how you feel."

"Will do. Night, O-man."

He waved at me and disconnected the call.

Next week would not get here fast enough for me to get to see him in person in Denver.

NINE

Oscar: I'm on the bumpiest flight ever. Have I mentioned I'm not a fan of turbulence?

Dixon: I wish I could hold your hand or something to distract you.

Oscar: This chatting is a good distraction. Somehow, Corey and Nate are both sleeping. I wish I had their ability to just doze off. Even on a smooth flight, it's impossible for me.

Dixon: I used to be that way. I think at some point it got so common for me to travel that it didn't matter anymore.

Oscar: And flying never made you anxious?

Dixon: Not that I remember. I think the first time I was on a plane was when Mom took me to camp in Michigan.

My face was plastered against the window the whole time because I didn't want to miss anything. I hated the seat belt because I couldn't sit like I wanted to.

Oscar: We were five that summer. Our first year to go to camps. I stayed closer to home, though. The first time I flew was the next summer when I went to Miami for the first time. I can't remember if I liked that or not. I just never traveled by plane much. Once we moved, I didn't fly again until I traveled with Miami Ballet when I was seventeen. That was a bumpy flight too, and I hated it. I tried to be cool because I didn't want to be the kid that freaked out.

Dixon: How was it you never came back to Wisconsin? You had grandparents in Madison.

Oscar: When you live in Miami, family in the north is more than happy to come visit during the winter.

Dixon: LOL. That totally makes sense.

Oscar: How are you feeling after practice?

Dixon: Today's pretty good. I'll play reduced time again tonight, but expect to be back to full on the road trip. But I'll probably keep a brace on it for another week or two.

Oscar: That's not bad, even though I know you hate the brace.

Dixon: I can't wait for that to go. It's just weird having it under the pads. Not at all comfortable. And I've had to get used to skating with it. I am glad I avoided IR though. I hate not playing at all, so just playing less is okay.

Oscar: Damn. I hate it when the plane jerks. You know that feeling when it seems to drop for a second, but then it jerks back up? I think my stomach has left the plane.

Dixon: Sorry. I promise if I was there, I wouldn't be asleep next to you. I'd do whatever you needed to keep you distracted.

Oscar: You won't go to sleep on me like these two? Do you see how Corey's leaning against the window? [Picture of Corey, face against the window with his mouth slightly open.] How can he do that? His head must knock into the window. And then Nate. He's so still, headphones on. [Picture of Nate sitting upright, eyes closed and headphones on.]

Dixon: Nope. I wouldn't leave you like that. I'd do whatever I could to help you be calm.

Oscar: Remember how great you were at that? That time I slept over at your house and there was that big storm in the middle of the night. I was terrified.

Dixon: Yes! We'd built a fort out of stuff in my room, and we were in sleeping bags. The storm woke us up. You looked so freaked out, but if I recall right, you were also trying to seem like you were keeping it together.

Oscar: Remember what I said about that trip when I was seventeen? I didn't want to be that kid. You were amazing, though. You decided we were going to build Lego spaceships, so you brought your giant tub of bricks into the fort.

Dixon: We were not good builders.

Oscar: No, we were not. We did our best, even if everything always looked like a square or rectangle. Still, we had fun trying, and it was a great distraction.

Dixon: You know, I've seen Lego vending machines in a couple of airports. You could get yourself something to build and keep it in your carry-on.

Oscar: I'll look out for one of those. In situations like this, I need more than trying to watch a movie or something. I tried to play a game on my phone, but the turbulence makes that more difficult. I wonder, do you think bricks would end up flying off my table?

Dixon: I don't know. I guess that would be a possibility. We'll have to take a flight together and figure that out.

Oscar: Do you think we'd travel together as well now as we did when we were kids?

Dixon: The actual travel part's got to be better. For starters, if we're in a car, we won't have to be in safety seats.

Oscar: LOL!

Dixon: And we can go anywhere we want. Not just where our parents take us.

Oscar: You're thinking of that orchard, aren't you?

Dixon: Yes! That was the worst. So boring.

Oscar: Except the donuts. Those were good.

Dixon: It didn't make up for all the walking around, looking at trees, and picking apples. We just wanted to hang around the animals, but our parents weren't having that.

Oscar: That was more of a you thing. That pig was scary the way it stared at me. I didn't want to be near it.

Dixon: Noted. We will not go to an orchard or to a place with scary pigs.

Oscar: Good! I'm going to have to go. My phone's about to die and my charger's in the overhead, so I can't get to it. The turbulence has calmed down, so hopefully they'll let us get up soon.

Dixon: Glad to hear it's calmer. Looking forward to talking later. And you could always wake up Nate and tell him I asked if he'd keep you distracted.

Oscar: Remember, I'm trying not to be that guy. LOL! Talk to you later. Have a good game!

TEN

OSCAR

Nerves vibrated through me. I'd swear a guitar had gotten lodged in my chest along with a tiny player who kept plucking on the tightly wound strings, sending waves of excitement, anxiety, anticipation, and who knew what else through me. I hadn't been this wound up since, with only a couple of hours' notice, I went on for a principal dancer in *Fancy Free* when I was nineteen.

I'd rehearsed plenty and had been in front of many audiences, but the sudden call and pressure from myself to get it right for my castmates had turned me into a mess. Luckily, the performance had gone flawlessly.

Dix and I had talked and texted nearly every day since I'd seen him in New York two weeks ago. I'd been a wreck all day knowing he was in the city. He'd arrived this afternoon and had gone straight to the rink for the game against Denver. We'd wished each other a good game and a good show. The game had started before the show, so I'd gotten to see some while I got ready. There hadn't been any goals scored by the time I'd had to go on stage.

Unless the game went to overtime, he'd said he should finish at nearly the same time I did. In a fluke of scheduling, we were at the same hotel and we'd planned to meet in the bar.

Only Nate picked up on my mood, which he'd gotten ridiculously good at. Thankfully, the rest of the cast didn't catch on. Or, if they did, they said nothing.

I'd convinced myself that the feelings mostly had to be simple eagerness to see Dix again. Seeing him in person tonight, however, meant I'd be confronted head-on by my feelings for him. They'd started in New York and built since then with all the talking and catching up on the highlights of the past years.

The quirk of a smile he got when he was amused gave me a rush every time I saw it on FaceTime. Then there were his eyes, streaked with lighter bits of brown and gold that in the right light made them sparkle.

No one knew I'd dreamed about Dix twice in the past few days. In one we were having a picnic, which had seemed quite random. The other was the kind of dream was probably the sexiest dream I'd ever had—and something I wanted to do in real life.

The picnic had intrigued me. Did we go as friends? Was it a date? Some specifics I remembered, like we'd had chicken salad sandwiches—a definite throwback to childhood because his mom had made those a lot. We'd worn each other's merch too. He'd been in a Miami City Ballet T-shirt and I'd sported a New York Empire one.

The more I replayed that, the more I thought maybe we'd gone past dating and had become more.

"You're going to be fine," Nate said as we got ready to greet the fans. Word had filtered back that the line was long at the stage door. By the end of the New York week, Nate and I had started going out together because there'd been requests for pictures with both of us.

"I know." I sighed, annoyed at my jitters. "Sorry, I'm bouncing off the walls."

"It's all good. From everything you've told me, I don't think you've got anything to worry about."

I picked up my phone from my makeup table and checked the game. It had ended while I was in the shower, and Dix would be in a good mood since New York had won by a goal. I shoved the phone in my jeans.

"We might have put too much pressure on ourselves in our chats." I poked at my hair, trying to get it right. The curls kept doing the wrong thing, not staying put. "Or at least I might have. We've each said, maybe too many times, how we're excited to see each other. What if it's all awkward silence?"

Nate put his coat on, and I decided my hair was as good as it would get. I wouldn't rush the time with the fans, but I wanted to be at the hotel too. At least it was within walking distance, so I didn't have to wait for a car.

"There won't be any kind of silence. You guys talk about so much—that's not just going to dry up when you're sitting at the same table." He clapped me on the shoulder.

"Just tell me I'm silly." I chuckled at myself.

"I'd call you crazy for him." He bugged his eyes out and made an O with his mouth. "Yeah, I said that."

I shook my head as I felt heat creep across my cheeks. Was I that obvious?

We grabbed our packs and headed out. My phone buzzed with a text, and I couldn't get the phone out of my pocket fast enough. I stopped us in the hall to read it.

Dixon: On my way to the hotel. Should be there in about twenty minutes.

I grinned as I typed.

Oscar: Headed out. Lots of fans tonight, so I'll be there as soon as I can.

Dixon: I'll be in the bar. Look forward to seeing you!

"That look on your face says it all. Come on." Nate gave me a playful shove down the hall. "Just be open to the possibilities, okay? It's too easy to focus on the reasons something may not work and use that as an easy out."

Nate had a point. The worst that could happen was that Dix and I fell out of touch again. So many other outstanding things *could* happen, though.

"Oh, Oscar, hey, I was hoping I'd catch you before you left." That voice, which was coming from behind me, stopped me cold. What was he doing here?

"Who's that?" Nate whispered as we turned to face

Tobias Clark. He and Alexi were coming out of the lounge.

"And Nathaniel too, fantastic."

Alexi stopped next to Tobias. "I'm going to let you three talk. I'll be in touch." He held up a business card. "It was good to meet you."

Tobias, who was decked out in an all-black suit, turned on his smile. I cringed. He wanted something.

"You too, Alexi. Talk soon." He walked the few steps to us. "Aren't you going to introduce us, Oscar?"

I couldn't be rude, even though I wanted to tell Tobias exactly where he could go. Even though it'd been more than five years since I last saw him, just being near Tobias made my temper flare. "Nate, this is a former cast-mate from Miami, Tobias Clark." I didn't keep the chill from my voice.

"Oh, come on, Oscar, we're more than that." Tobias ignored my disdain and stepped forward to shake Nate's hand. "It's good to meet you, Nate. That was a spectac-ular performance tonight."

"Thank you."

"Listen, I won't keep you since you've got fans wait-ing." He produced another couple of business cards from his pants pocket. "I'm starting a new company here in Denver and I'd love to talk with you about the vision I have for it and why I think you'd be a great fit."

Nate took the card and glanced at it. "Thank you. I'll pass this on to my agent. She's the one you should talk to. But I'll tell you that I'm very happy based in New York and not looking to move."

I recognized the flash of disappointment in Tobias's eyes. "If not as a permanent company member, perhaps you'll join us as a guest artist." He leveled his gaze at me. "Oscar, I'd love to bring you into the company. You've grown so much since I saw you last. Tonight was absolutely stunning."

"Thanks."

I wouldn't tell him here that was the last thing I would ever do. I took a card and slipped it into my pocket, hoping that was it. Fans and Dix were waiting, and I wasn't sure how much longer I could be nice.

"Can we talk while you're in town? I'm meeting some of the other dancers over the next few days."

"My schedule's pretty tight. I don't think I can."

That was a lie. My schedule was no tighter than Nate's or anyone else's.

"Okay," he said, voice tinged with a bit of frustration. "Well, the invitation stands."

That wasn't the answer he'd expected.

"We should go." Nate pulled out the Sharpie he kept in his coat pocket for extra effect.

"Let's get to it." I turned to go.

"It was good to meet you, Tobias." Nate was more gracious than I could be.

"Oscar, I really hope you'll call," Tobias called out as we walked away. "And it was good to meet you too, Nate."

Nate didn't break stride but turned briefly to wave to Tobias.

"I take it there's a story there," Nate whispered as we turned a corner.

"Oh yeah. He's an asshole ex."

"I thought he might be something like that based on his quip about being more than a castmate." He stashed the business card in his coat pocket. "I suspect Audrey will never, ever see that card."

"You don't have to do that on my account."

We stopped in the small lobby before we went out.

"I don't want to work with people who can be called asshole. And besides, he came across like a sketchy salesman."

I grunted. There was really nothing to say about that.

"And we'll just leave it at that." He shot me a grin.

I took a deep breath and let it out slowly. The surprise of seeing Tobias was in the past now. Some great fans awaited, and then I'd see Dix.

I pushed open the stage door to a burst of applause from the people who were huddled around. The cold had become sharper since I'd arrived at the theater, but it didn't keep these people from being here. Two other guys were out here talking and signing. It was a party atmosphere, and it was just what I needed to shake the irritation of seeing Tobias.

ELEVEN

DIXON

The team bus drove by the theater on the way to the hotel. It took a lot of willpower not to beg to be let off at the red light to wait for Oscar.

As soon as we arrived, I headed up to my room, which already had my bag in it courtesy of the equipment team. I organized my toiletries in the bathroom and situated a few things that would make both going to bed and waking up easier. It also meant things were tidy if I had company.

With that done, I headed to the bar to find a good place to stake out the entrance and wait for Oscar. I'd stayed in the suit since he'd said he liked how I looked dressed up.

I settled into a corner table and ordered cranberry juice, one of my favorite postgame drinks, and chicken fingers.

Since the game's final buzzer, first date jitters had racked me—even if we weren't officially calling this a date. Still, I had the same anxiety I'd had when Tyrone asked me out at high school graduation and I'd said yes. The date that followed had scared me because it was a first after staying mostly in the closet. I'd only come out the summer before, and then it'd been to select friends. Tyrone had been the brave one, asking me out without knowing if I was gay or not. He'd called it a graduation present to himself to see what would happen.

Wanting to date Oscar—though I wasn't sure we could even call it dating since we lived in different states —was a huge deal. I had doubts about the practicality, and even the ramifications of trying. Despite it all, I couldn't talk myself out of it.

At least that was what the loudest parts of me said. I had a lot of voices in my head with different opinions. What was the Disney movie with all the emotions vying for control? I had far more than five demanding to be heard.

We'd both said things that made it sound like we wanted to give a relationship a try. Tonight would either kick-start a new phase or make it clear we'd only be friends.

Meanwhile, the thump in my chest provided a percussive beat as if I'd just come off the ice now rather than an hour ago. Could a heart explode from antic-ipation?

As the server brought my juice, Oscar and Nate walked into the lobby talking animatedly. Oscar's gaze quickly found mine, and he sent me a smile that warmed me through. Almost as quickly, though, his expression clouded and so did Nate's as another man approached. He wasn't one of their castmates. Since Nate and Oscar seemed to know him, I guessed he was someone with the show.

I sipped my drink and watched, though I couldn't see much of Oscar because of where the stranger stood. Nate placed a hand on Oscar's arm and looked like he was ready to go. A debate raged in my head—should I go over there? Did they need help? I wanted a clue from them because I didn't want to interrupt and possibly make a mess of things.

Luckily, I didn't have to make the choice. The man stepped aside, and Oscar and Nate headed toward the bar. Oscar shot me an eye roll but no smile. The man looked exasperated, crossing his arms over his chest as he watched them go.

Nate and Oscar came into the bar. I only had eyes for Oscar, though, as he dodged around tables and people with a gracefulness I hadn't noticed the last time we were together. On stage he moved beautifully, and he walked that way too.

I stood as they approached, which got Oscar's smile to come out. He came right up to me and I opened my arms for him.

We embraced.

He squeezed me tight.

I relished the contact as his body pressed into mine.

"Hey. Sorry to keep you waiting. That took longer than expected." He kissed me on the cheek and released me.

I didn't let him go.

Should I kiss him back?

He looked at me, an eyebrow raised.

Oh no.

That kiss had overloaded my brain. Small, sweet, but also *everything*.

I let him go and stepped back to give us space.

"Uhm. Yeah. No. Not long at all. Only just now got my drink." I struggled to recover from feeling him against me like that and realized I'd ignored Nate. "Hi, I'm Dix. It's great to finally meet you, Nate."

"You too." We traded smiles since Oscar was between us. "I promise I'm not crashing your time together. I'm just finishing the story that we had someone to meet."

"Sorry about that," Oscar said. "Thanks for playing along."

"What was that? I almost came over there because it looked sort of confrontational."

Oscar sighed. He didn't want to tell this story. "That's Tobias Clark. He used to dance with Miami, and now apparently he's artistic director of a new company that will also feature him"—Oscar sighed again—"and he's an ex. Sorry you had to hear about him like that. We haven't really had the ex talk yet."

A knot formed in my stomach. I wasn't sure if I should ask more or not, but before I could decide, the question spilled out. "He wants you two to work with him?"

"Yeah. But no way." Oscar's nostrils flared, and my

pang of jealousy retreated. He did not like this Tobias guy.

"Enough about him," Nate said. "Don't let him spoil your evening. And I'm going to go so I'm not your third wheel." He gave a quick hug to Oscar. "I'll see you later." Then he gave me a quick hug too. "Dix, I'm glad we met."

"Me too. Have a good night, Nate."

He headed across the lobby to the elevators.

Oscar sat down and I fumbled my stool, knocking it backward and into the wall. I cringed at the noise, even though no one else seemed to notice. The kiss kept rolling over in my brain, making me way too flustered.

Should I have kissed him back?

Would I have the chance again?

I was terrible at this. Oscar seemed so smooth and confident. How could I possibly get this right?

"Congrats on the win." The sweet looks from him continued to wreak havoc on my ability to respond.

"Thanks," I finally sputtered as I sat down. "Probably shouldn't say that too loudly in enemy territory, but it was satisfying since they beat us at home earlier in the season."

The server brought the chicken strips and set them between us.

"I ordered a snack. I checked and they don't have pancakes this time of night, so I picked something we could share."

"Perfect. Can I get some ginger ale?"

"Of course." The server scurried away.

"I saw you and Nate talking to people when our bus went by. You weren't kidding about the crowd."

"Yeah. They were another incredible audience."

I nodded. "And you never have people booing you like we did tonight."

"Right." He chuckled and spun the silver ring that was on the middle finger of his right hand. Had he worn that in New York? "I'd be so mortified if that happened. How do you deal with that?"

"Well, if we're on the road, it means we're doing the job right. It sucks, though, if you get boos from your home crowd."

"Speaking of on the road, I can't believe you didn't tell me your Dallas game was an afternoon one. I'm getting a ticket. Nate might come along too."

The pounding of my heart picked up again with renewed intensity, like a bunch of anxious players banging their sticks against the boards.

"Is it? Sorry. I don't pay attention until closer to the game. When we're traveling, it's all about being where they tell me to be and I don't have the detailed itinerary for next week yet. Let me hook you up with some good tickets."

"You don't have to do that." His tone shifted to more guarded. "I can get one as soon as Nate decides if—"

"I'd like to, though. I got to see you from a good seat. Let me get you a good one for this."

He nodded, and his sweet smile reappeared. Damn if he wasn't doing a number on me. All I wanted to do was touch him, but I kept that under wraps since I didn't know if he wanted that. I thought he did, but...

Argh. Why was this so hard?

"I can't wait to see you zip down the ice. I remember how slow you used to be and how often you'd leave the puck behind."

"Hey now." His walk down memory lane scattered my overthinking—at least for the moment. "Two can play that game. I recall a *Three Little Pigs* where you lost your balance and caused a house to fall down."

He hid his face in his hands for a moment as he shook his head. "I'm glad you didn't see my gangly adolescent years. God, I don't know how they didn't throw me out of the school because of all the awkwardness."

Oscar focused his gaze on me. I felt very seen but also studied like he could suddenly see and know everything about me.

"I don't see any awkward now." My voice dropped to nearly a whisper as I focused on him. The rest of the bar faded away, like someone had changed a camera lens so Oscar had all the focus.

"I'd like to go on an actual date with you." He took my hand in his. The heat of the touch rushed up my arm and threatened to crash my brain again. "There. I said it. I actually think we've both wanted to say it for days."

"Yeah." I nodded as I heard the relief in my voice. Thank God he'd had the balls to speak the words. "Even though I have no idea how we plan it, but yes. I want that. I haven't felt this connected to someone—honestly, maybe ever. And I'm pretty sure it's more than friendship talking."

"It might be crazy, but I want to see what happens." He grabbed a chicken tender, dipped it in the barbecue sauce, and took a bite.

"What if—"

"Uh-uh." His voice was gentle and his expression was about as kind as I imagined it could get. "I've thought about that too, and I'd rather fail than wonder about the possibilities."

His confidence inspired me. While anxiety still nagged at me, surrendering to the desire to know Oscar more overrode it.

"A date it is then."

"Cheers to the future date night." Oscar raised his ginger ale and held it out over the chicken strips. I clicked my glass against his and we drank.

I HOPED that had come off as calmly and coolly as I'd wanted it to.

At least I hadn't embarrassed myself, which had been a real concern. That guitar in my chest was playing a much softer strum since I'd gotten past telling him that.

"I'm glad you settled that." Dix sounded relieved. Had he gotten as anxious as I had? "I'm terrified we're going to end up hurt, which means we probably wouldn't have a friendship anymore either." He paused and scrubbed his hand across his beard. "I know that's possible even if we're in the same city, but long distance seems…"

We might be too much alike. That same thing had crossed my mind numerous times in the past week, often leading to thoughts that would just trail off.

I shook my head. "I have to come clean. That may have sounded confident, but I'm worried. Or maybe not worried, I'm... hell, I don't know. Concerned? But I want to believe it'll be awesome and I'd rather focus on that."

"I like that."

Dix reached for another piece of chicken and dipped it into the sauce. As he brought it to his mouth, it started to drip. He darted his tongue out and caught the drop before it released.

Of course, I couldn't help but imagine him licking me, even though it wasn't the best time for those thoughts. Sometimes my brain had terrible timing.

"You helped me kick my concerns to the curb, at least for now," Dix said as he cleaned his hands with a napkin. "We're adults. We're athletes. We know how to do awesome."

"So I might as well tell you about Tobias." It was as good a time as any to talk about the past since it had confronted me earlier. "He's my longest relationship at just over four years, and I let that go on longer than I should've. We met when he joined Miami. I was barely 19. Before him, I dated a few people and had some friends with benefits during school."

The server silently swooped in with drink refills. I appreciated that he didn't interrupt.

Dix's brow furrowed in deep thought, and even though he seemed on the verge of speaking a few times, he didn't.

I wanted to know what he was thinking, though. "You can say whatever's on your mind. It's okay."

"Did he hurt you?" Dix's tone carried a sharp edge to it.

"Not physically. Mentally, a little, but I'm way over it now. Whenever something good happened in my career, he had a knack for trying to bring me down. If I got a role that wasn't what I wanted, he'd list off reasons why he thought I wasn't good enough. Even when I'd get praise in class, he'd later nitpick and point out areas he thought I should improve. The self-doubt nearly derailed me, but a couple of close friends helped me see his manipulation. I broke up with him and then kept my distance, which wasn't easy since he stayed with the company for another year."

"What a jerk. I'm glad you have friends who look out for you."

"Me too. It turned out that I wasn't the only one he played mind games with. As we all started talking about it, more and more often no one wanted to work with him. He'll deny it, I'm sure, but I believe the backlash he faced was the reason he left Miami. I can't imagine what it would be like to work for him unless he's changed in the past five years."

"Please tell me you have better collaborators now." Dix watched me closely as if to make sure he didn't need to come to my defense. It was a sexy look, even if I didn't need protection.

"One hundred percent. I love the people I work with in Miami and the people on this tour. I refuse to work with people who aren't kind. While I appreciate intensity and a desire for excellence, I won't tolerate anyone who belittles or mistreats anyone. Thankfully, it hasn't come to having to turn down projects."

"Are you going to warn your castmates about Tobias?" Dix's eyes tracked something happening behind me. He caught my questioning look when his gaze came back to me. "He just sat down with Corey."

A sigh escaped before I could stop it. "I'm tempted. But I also don't want to interfere if he has somehow changed. I'm going to talk to Nate about it since he already knows the story." I took a quick drink and decided to get the spotlight off me for a bit. "Tell me a little about your dating past."

"My first date was right after high school graduation. We went out a few times that summer but then went our separate ways. There was some dating in college but not much because I focused on hockey and classes. That changed at the start of junior year when I met Colin. He was in the marching band, and we were both on campus early for practices."

Dix sounded almost clinical as he recounted the story.

"I didn't object when Colin suggested, as graduation got closer, that we were just a school thing." His cool facade broke a bit as he furrowed his brow and sounded frustrated. "I suppose I should've had more intense feelings about it. Since I didn't, it was probably good that we didn't even try to take it further. Since then there's been some casual dates, but no one ever quite clicked."

I ran my hand through my hair and caught a spark in Dix's eye that seemed to come out of nowhere.

He looked into his cranberry juice and stirred it with the straw before focusing back on me. "I already feel more comfortable and in sync with you than anyone else."

My heart melted, and I knew my declaration about dating had been right.

"So do I." We stared at each other, and our smiles widened. "Now we have to figure out what an actual date looks like." I took another piece of chicken and flashed back to that drop of sauce Dix had licked off his last piece. "Any chance we could do something in Dallas?"

"Let me see." He pulled out his phone and tapped and swiped the screen. After a moment, he sighed. "Odds are we'll leave after the game since we're headed back to New York and an off day."

"Oh well, it was worth trying. Still love that I get to catch the game, though."

"Actually, we might be able to have breakfast. I'll know in the next few days what the full schedule is."

"I'll take whatever time with you that I can have—my newly minted boyfriend."

Boyfriend had just slipped out. But I didn't regret saying it either.

At least I'd managed to say it with some of that fake confidence I'd had before.

"Please, say it again."

Did he shudder?

"My newly minted boyfriend." I tried to say it in exactly the same tone.

Dix's gaze burned into me as the tip of his tongue darted out to moisten his lips. "I like it when my boyfriend calls me his boyfriend."

I calmly got up from my seat and crossed to his side of the table. Being at a high top was perfect because the stool put him at just the right level for me to easily kiss him.

As I placed my hands on both sides of his face, the softest moan escaped him when my lips touched his. We kissed and I flushed with excitement.

I had a boyfriend. And I'd just given him more than a kiss on the cheek.

As much as I wanted to ask him to take me to his room, I kept my libido in check. We didn't need to go too fast.

"You've got three more weeks, right?" Dix asked through a smile when he pulled back.

"Yeah. Dallas, San Diego, and Seattle."

"What happens after that? Back to the regular job?"

I pulled my stool around so I could sit closer. "I'm taking a couple of weeks off to settle back in at home and then, yeah, back at it with the company."

"We should figure out if we can be together at least some of that time."

"I'd be good with fourteen days of kissing?"

Dix hummed again. Was that one of his things? I liked it.

"And maybe more?" His eyes sparkled with mischief. Maybe I wasn't the only one struggling to keep things from going too fast.

My mind raced to decide what to say. "We've got some time now."

Maybe we could go a little faster.

Another hum, this time accompanied by widened eyes. He raised his hand and caught the attention of our server, who immediately came over. "Can I get the check, please?"

"Certainly. I'll be right back."

"What did you have in mind for more?" The lilt Dix put on *more* shot through me, sending tingles throughout my chest.

"More kisses?"

He nodded as the server returned. I pulled my wallet from my pants, ready to pay.

"It's all set for your signature to charge to your room."

"Thank you very much." Dix looked it over, added the tip, and scrawled his signature across the slip of paper. He handed it back, and the server wished us a good night.

"What do I owe you?"

He shook his head. "Don't worry about it. It's taken care of."

"Thanks." I pocketed my wallet. "Next one's on me, though, since you bought the pancakes too."

He stood and I followed suit.

"That works."

As I turned, I found Tobias staring at me as Corey talked to him. Dix took my hand in his, and those feelings I'd had bloomed into full swooning. Hand in hand felt so right.

"My room okay for that kissing?" he asked quietly.

"Lead the way."

We headed for the elevators in silence, though still connected by our hands.

"You're sure this is okay?" I had to double-check.

"Yes. Very much yes."

"Cool." I pushed the up button. "I didn't want you to feel pressured."

He brought our hands up and placed a kiss on mine.

"I've wanted this since New York."

My cheeks heated as I remembered how badly I'd wanted his kisses that night.

I craned my neck up and kissed his lips lightly.

"Who was your first kiss?" I couldn't resist the question.

"Tyrone. The same guy I mentioned before. Talk about somebody with confidence. He'd asked me out, planned the date to the movies where we made out a bit in the back row. I was too scared to enjoy it, but I got better as the summer went on. What about you?"

We got to his room, and he waved his phone at the lock. I opened the door with my free hand.

"Truth or dare when I was fourteen. Teresa decided I had to kiss Brady, and I was happy to do it because I had a secret crush on him. Brady was a couple of years older and already out as bi. He was a great kisser too."

The door clicked shut behind us.

Dix stood before me, his hand still holding onto mine. With his other hand, he gently cupped the back of my head and brushed his lips over mine. In response I pressed my lips to his, wrapping my arm around his waist to pull us closer together. Our kiss deepened as he explored my mouth with his tongue.

The kiss sent a surge of energy through me, and I couldn't hold back a shudder. It'd been so long since I'd been kissed like that that I'd forgotten how mind-altering it could be.

When we finally caught our breath, Dix had a smile as wide as mine.

"I'm definitely glad we came up here," I said as I led him over to the couch.

He sat down and guided me to sit on him. I positioned my legs to straddle his hips and pressed my body against his as I went in for another kiss.

He caressed my back as I adjusted myself to find the perfect position. Without words, we knew exactly what we desired as our kisses varied between gentle and passionate.

He must have felt my hard dick pressing into him because I was very aware of his as it occasionally pulsed. But we kept our attention on our kisses. I couldn't get enough of Dix's hands on me. Even through my clothes, every spot his fingers touched begged for more.

We spent over an hour on the couch exploring each other before I caught the time on the clock. It was past one. Even though we both needed sleep, it took us a while to finally say goodnight and for me to go back to my room.

I looked forward to whatever time we'd get to spend together in Dallas.

Oscar: Check out this amazing sunrise.

Dixon: Oh wow. That's gorgeous. Look at all that color with the pinks and purples. You're already on the way to the TV station, aren't you? The hotel didn't have that view.

Oscar: Yeah, we're almost there. And Nate says hello.

Dixon: Hi Nate! I'm beginning to wonder if you have my phone bugged or something. This is the second time since I saw you where I pick up the phone to text you and you make it vibrate in my hand.

Oscar: I can think of better things to vibrate.

Dixon: Ha.

Oscar: What? It's true.

Dixon: You know, ever since we made out the other night, you've demonstrated a bit of a naughty streak. I like it.

Oscar: You bring it out.

Dixon: I'll do what I can to coax it out even more. I was about to text you to wish you a good TV appearance and to check on your ankle?

Oscar: The ankle is much better. This morning it just feels stiff. I see the doctor in a few hours. I'm hoping I get fully cleared. Don't get me wrong, I'm glad I've been able to still dance with Nate, but I hate not being able to perform the entire show.

Dixon: I wish I could kiss it and make it all better.

Oscar: I can think of more interesting places to kiss.

Dixon: Naughty boy.

Oscar: Who? Me? Maybe.

Dixon: Do you think we've jinxed ourselves somehow? I got hurt, then you get hurt a week later. We both had to sit out for a few days.

Oscar: I'm sure the universe has better things to do than mess with us.

Dixon: As long as it doesn't happen again.

Oscar: Fair enough. If it does, I'll make sure to file a complaint.

Dixon: LOL.

Oscar: What's the worst injury you've had playing?

Dixon: Had to be that injury in high school that kept me out six weeks. Since I went pro, the worst was when I twisted my knee last year and was out for two weeks. After that, I still played reduced time for another week. I hated every second.

Oscar: I don't know how you don't get hurt every single game.

Dixon: Padding! But I also don't know how you don't come down wrong more often. All those jumps and stuff. Figure skaters, gymnasts, high jumpers too. It's beyond me.

Oscar: Practice. Like anything else. I got hurt so much while I worked to increase my height in grand jetés.

Dixon: I imagine a lengthy conversation in our future catching up on years of injuries.

Oscar: LOL. I've got tons of stories. What's your day look like?

Dixon: At the moment, I'm waiting on the dryer to finish because it's Friday morning laundry time. We've got a light workout this morning and a team meeting. And, of course, a game tonight. What's going on for you besides TV and the doctor?

Oscar: Nate and I want to check out a place near the hotel that specializes in grilled cheese sandwiches. That'll be lunch.

Dixon: Want! One of my go-to comfort foods. I'll expect a full report.

Oscar: I'll send pictures with our review. We've also got a student performance this afternoon for some high school kids. Even if I'm cleared for tonight, I'll just be a host for that so that I don't put extra stress on the ankle.

Dixon: Sounds like a good day.

Oscar: I don't see why not. You should find somewhere new for your postgame meal and tell me about it.

Dixon: Hmm. I like that idea. It's been a while since I've tried a new place.

Oscar: Easy to understand since you've got the diner across the street.

Dixon: There is a new Mexican place I run by all the time and it's always busy.

Oscar: You can't go wrong with a tasty burrito or taco.

Dixon: Truth! It's been too long since I've had good carnitas. The place I used to get my fix closed more than a year ago.

Oscar: Even more reason for you to go there. By the way, I've got a carnitas tamales recipe from one of my tías that is insanely delicious. I'll make it for you sometime.

Dixon: That sounds amazing. I've added that to our list of future things to do. I'll make dessert.

Oscar: Oooh. What's on your dessert menu?

Dixon: I've pretty much nailed my mom's mint chocolate pie.

Oscar: For real? The one she'd make at Christmas?

Dixon: Yeah! You remember?

Oscar: Just like the pancakes, I absolutely remember that pie. I always wanted her to make it more than just at the holidays.

Dixon: Well, I make it a lot, more than I should. You'll be able to have your fill. The only reason I don't make it all the time is because the team nutritionist won't allow an all pie diet.

Oscar: Maybe just once we can have pie for dinner and eat our fill.

Dixon: We can do that. And don't think I haven't. That's what the off season is for!

Oscar: I've got to go. We've arrived at the station.

Dixon: Thanks for spending the ride with me and for the picture.

Oscar: Anytime! Talk to you tonight? Usual time?

Dixon: Should be, yeah. Let's text each other when we're home. Hope you dazzle Denver's morning TV watchers.

Oscar: We will! We've got a trimmed down version of the opening number to wake people up. And then a few other things we'll do in and out of the commercials. Nate and I will do a 30 second snippet from ours. It's the first time any of it will have been on TV.

Dixon: Cool! Send me links if it ends up online.

Oscar: Will do.

Dixon: And text me what the doctor says.

Oscar: Will do! Have a great day. Talk to you later.

FOURTEEN

DIXON

"Listen up, guys," Larry, one of our equipment managers, shouted from the doorway to the locker room. I hustled to get dressed because I wanted to grab maximum time with Oscar in the VIP lounge before I'd have to get on the bus for the airport. "We're not able to get out tonight. The storm in the Northeast has us grounded until morning."

Groans reverberated through the room. Suppressing a yelp of excitement, I considered the possibility of spending time with Oscar if he was free after his show tonight.

"Sorry. I know it's not what you wanted to hear." Larry waited for the murmurs to die out. "We're sorting out hotels and we'll let you know when we're ready to leave the arena."

A few guys, including me, thanked them as they retreated to work on logistics. The team's job wasn't easy, getting us moved around. Being stuck here overnight only made it harder. Thankfully, we didn't have a home game tomorrow.

I slipped on my suit jacket as many of my teammates got on their phones to break the news to loved ones. Meanwhile, time to tell mine the good news. We hadn't been able to do breakfast as our schedules had conspired against us, so this was a great bonus.

As I passed Caleb, he gave me a grin and a thumbs-up while keeping up his conversation with Dimitri. He knew Oscar was here, as I'd pointed him out during the game since his seats were behind our bench.

In the lounge, I found Oscar and Nate sitting on one of the comfy oversized couches. They were laughing at something on Nate's phone. Suddenly, Oscar looked up as if sensing my presence. His face lit up with joy as he stood. No one had ever looked at me with such warmth before, and it filled me with love.

"So happy to see you." Oscar wrapped his arms around me and we shared a kiss.

We kept the greeting PG rated for the lounge, even though every part of me wanted to keep him in my arms and our lips locked.

"That was intense, being so up close. Thanks for the incredible seats."

"Yeah, the best. Thanks for a fun afternoon. I totally get why Todd likes the game so much. It's great to see you again, Dixon." Nate and I traded a quick, friendly hug.

"You too, Nate. I wish we'd managed to win while you guys were here, though."

They shrugged.

"Whatever." Oscar sounded unconcerned about the loss. "The game's more exciting than I remember."

"There's something to be said about skating a lot faster and not being in a pack of kids just following the puck around."

I chuckled, remembering all too well what that was like.

"You look like you're having such a great time when you're on the ice. I swear you always came back to the bench with a huge grin." Oscar smiled a wide, toothy smile as if to demonstrate.

"I think it was more like this actually." Nate's smile was even bigger and more exaggerated.

Oscar looked closely as Nate held the expression. "Yeah. That's it."

They cracked themselves up, and I joined in. They'd formed such a tight friendship on the road, and I loved seeing parts of that.

"My job is to play. Don't get me wrong, I want to win. But if it ever gets to where I'm not having fun, it'll probably be time for me to hang it up." I reached out and hooked two of my fingers around two of Oscar's because I yearned for his touch. "So we're stuck here because of a storm."

Oscar's eyes lit up like I'd given him the best present. The look filled me with so much love. I hadn't known I could feel this way, and I wanted it to continue forever.

"I was thinking I could try to get a ticket to your show and, if you want, we could get together after."

"Yes, I want. Yes, please." He kept his voice at a low

level, but it was obvious he wanted to be louder. The smolder in his eyes was beyond sexy. "I heard we're sold out, but let me see what I can do."

"Don't worry about it, especially not this close to showtime. I can sort out something. Or I can be your biggest fan waiting for you at the stage door."

Oscar waved his phone in between us. "It's no bother. It's cool that we can see each other work on the same day." He talked and texted. "Where are you staying tonight?"

"No idea. People are making phone calls."

"I can make myself scarce if you need me to," Nate said.

Oscar and I shook our heads.

"I might steal him away from you tonight, though."

Spending the entire night with Oscar would be incredible. We hadn't taken that leap in Denver, but maybe we could here.

"I suppose I could go one night without him in the room."

"There." Oscar slipped his phone in the pocket of his jacket. "We'll see what's possible. Would you be willing to hang backstage or something? I asked if they'd allow that."

"That'd be an interesting perspective. I'll watch from wherever you can put me."

He nodded. I appreciated the lengths he was going to to make sure I could see the show. However, while I wanted to see him perform again, I couldn't wait to get to the postshow time.

"As for after, I'd love to have a sleepover."

Warmth washed over me. Thank God I hadn't over-stepped with what I'd said to Nate. Before I could say anything, Oscar's phone vibrated loudly and he grabbed for it. He hummed as he read.

"They'll have information for you at guest services."

After New York, I'd never expected to see his show again. The thought of experiencing Oscar and Nate's artistry again thrilled me. This time I'd remember Kleenex.

I gathered him into a hug. "I appreciate this so much. Please thank whoever is making it happen."

I savored the feeling of Oscar against me. I didn't want to let him go, especially when he nuzzled his head against my shoulder.

"I'm sorry to break this up, but we should get going," Nate said quietly.

I released Oscar, and we held each other's gaze. He gave me a look mixed with kindness, happiness, and a tinge of longing.

"I'm glad we'll have time together tonight," I finally said.

"Me too."

As we stood there, the desire I had for Oscar seemed to grow stronger. It was as if our bond strengthened as we made the evening's plans.

Nate continued to be the responsible one. "A car is close by. Only five minutes away."

"I'll hang out with you while you wait." I gestured for Oscar and Nate to go into the corridor. "Maybe I wished so hard to get more time with you I helped create the storm."

"Maybe we combined powers." His sly smile went beyond cute. "There's a great diner by the theatre and we've become obsessed with their mac and cheese."

"Oh my God, yes." Nate's eyes fluttered closed as if he were reliving the flavors. "We've already eaten there three times despite the crazy amount of carbs."

"Are you asking me to dinner?"

"Hey, Dixon." Caleb approached from the locker room, decked out in his game day suit. "This must be Oscar."

"It is. Oscar, this is Caleb, friend and team captain. And this is Oscar's friend and dance partner, Nate."

"Great to meet you," Caleb said as he exchanged handshakes with them.

"You too," Oscar said. "I've heard all about you from Dix."

"All good I hope."

"For sure."

"Sorry we showed you a loss."

"It was still a blast to watch you guys play."

"I loved it," Nate added.

"You guys able to get together since we're stuck for the night?" Caleb looked between Oscar and me.

"We are," Oscar said. "He's coming to the show, and we just made dinner plans."

"At least someone's happy with the weather." Caleb clapped me on the back.

Heat rose in my cheeks. I had nothing to be embarrassed about and yet there it was.

Nate's phone buzzed in his hand, and he stole a look at the display.

"I guess that's our car." Oscar looked to Nate for confirmation and got a nod in return. "Caleb, I hope we can hang out sometime."

"That would be great. Aaron would love to get everyone in the same place, though that may not happen until the off season. Nate, maybe you and Todd can join us as well? I know six schedules might be a challenge, but let's try to make it happen."

Nate looked surprised, and I was too. I'd mentioned to Caleb that Nate's husband was envious that he was coming to the game today, but I didn't expect Caleb to remember that and even extend an invite.

"We would love that. Thank you."

"You guys should get out of here. Have a great show tonight." Caleb clapped me on the shoulder again as he headed to wherever he was going.

I followed Oscar and Nate. "Do you know where you're going?" I asked because I didn't.

"Yeah," Oscar said. "When we came back here, we asked the best place to grab a car."

"Smart."

We arrived at a small reception area that reminded me of the place I'd checked in to see Oscar at the stage door. A member of the Stars staff sat at the desk. Outside, a Lyft waited.

"Text me when you can and let me know what's

going on." Oscar leaned in and placed his lips on mine for another gentle kiss. "I'll see you in a few hours."

I wrapped him in a quick hug. "I can't wait."

One more quick peck on my cheek and he was out the door with Nate. They waved as they got in the car.

I sighed quietly as I watched them pull away. Bad weather couldn't have come at a better time.

FIFTEEN
OSCAR

There was an indescribable energy in me tonight, brought on by Dix being in the audience. My fellow cast-mates also noticed. I received compliments on my performance multiple times throughout the night. The most meaningful one came from Nate, who said he almost cried during our pas de deux.

The crew had come through big time, finding a place for Dix to watch. Rather than backstage, which probably would've been a distraction for me, they'd allowed him to hang out with the lighting and sound team at the back of the theater.

He'd texted at intermission and raved about being there and seeing some of the behind-the-scenes stuff too.

Time had moved at a snail's pace, though, from the moment I'd left Dix at the arena.

Even though the show was exhilarating, it seemed to take an eternity to get through the two hours.

There was still the crowd at the stage door too. As

much as I loved the audience, I wanted to get on with the night.

Dix and I had only a few hours to spend together, and the ticking clock echoed in my head.

It occurred to me while changing that the elusive first date might be about to happen. We knew New York and Denver hadn't been it. But we'd hastily arranged tonight, just like NYC.

I wasn't sure I actually cared about the date designation anymore. What mattered was being with Dix, whether we were doing something exciting or simply relaxing.

Our daily FaceTime conversations had only intensified my longing. His piercing eyes, even through the screen, seemed to see right into me. Not only did he see me, but he cared for me in ways I'd never experienced before. His genuine concern for my ankle injury and the unwavering support when I'd faced Tobias in Denver were just a few examples that showed who he was.

Our relationship so far had similarities to creating a dance. Often the act of creation unlocked something in my soul I hadn't realized I'd sealed. The more I reconnected with Dix, the more I cast off any doubts.

But I longed for more than stolen moments via text or phone or FaceTime or whatever. Actually spending time *with* each other mattered, and for more than a few hours. I wanted days.

Maybe when the tour was done, I could spend most of my time off in New York. Even if Dix was in practice and game mode, there'd be more time together. Summer had possibilities too. We'd have to figure out where to spend it.

I wanted to know if I was right that we were couple material.

Coupledom was where I wanted to be—where I was sure we could be.

The thing about tonight's show, which I probably wouldn't tell anyone, was that during the pas de deux, I envisioned Dixon. The dance was our life together rather than the fictional characters Nate and I had dreamed up. Not only had Nate almost cried, I almost had too with all the feels colliding.

Dix texted that he was in the green room and I sped up getting ready to leave. I'd brought dressier postshow clothes—nice black jeans and an indigo blue sweater I looked good in.

"You about ready to go?" Nate poked his head in my dressing room. In this theater, for the first time on the tour, the eight of us had our own rooms.

"Yup." I stood and slipped on my coat.

When we got to the green room, Dix was chatting with two men.

He smiled as we approached. A range of emotions flickered across his face, and he seemed pleased with what he saw. My dick noticed his interest and pulsed in my jeans. I willed it to behave as I didn't need to do the autograph line with a hard-on.

"O-man! Great show tonight. I swear you're all next level from when I saw you in New York, especially you and Nate." Dix seemed like he had more to say but stopped short. "I'm so sorry. My manners flew out the window. Oscar, Nate, this is Kenneth and Chester. They're New York fans and we got to talking about the game. They're patrons here."

"You were incredible tonight," Chester said. "I've never seen anything quite like your pas de deux. Simply stunning." He held up his program and a Sharpie. "Would you mind signing?"

I grinned, most likely a goofy one. I couldn't help it with Dix just inches away and looking fabulous in his dark gray game day suit punctuated with a dark purple shirt and tie.

"Of course. I'm really glad you enjoyed the performance." I talked and signed, a bit of multitasking I'd gotten used to. "Like Dixon said, it continues to evolve and tonight the audience was so good."

I handed the program and pen over to Nate.

"Everyone was so invested in it." Nate also knew how to sign and carry a conversation. "There were times I heard gasps from the stage and even some crying. And such a kind ovation too."

"Y'all deserved it," Kenneth said. "And it was great to see one of our own dancers up there. We love Alexi and this was different than what he does with the company here."

Nate handed back the program.

"Thank you so much," Chester said. "Hope you enjoy your night."

"Next time New York's in town, we'll get tickets to come watch you too," Kenneth added.

"I look forward to it."

Nate, Dix, and I left the green room, heading for the exit. "So, where did you end up staying?"

"The downtown Marriott. The team's split up in three different hotels."

Nate and I traded looks and chuckled.

"What?" Dix looked adorably befuddled.

"We're at the same hotel. Again."

"The travel gods really like you two," Nate said.

Dix leaned in for a quick kiss before we stepped out to greet the waiting fans. Nate and I went about our usual routine while Dix found a spot to wait. Once again he was awesome, managing to be in my line of sight, usually smiling.

"What are you up to now?" Dix asked Nate as we joined him after we'd talked to the last person.

"Headed back to the room to call home. I'm severely missing my guy tonight. I hope you enjoy the mac and cheese. Hopefully, we haven't oversold it."

"If Oscar says it's good, I believe him. His mom is a master chef with anything that involves noodles and cheese."

"Just like your mom with breakfast," Oscar added.

"Sounds like you're set then. I hope you guys have a great night." Nate didn't miss a beat, heading off to the hotel.

I took Dix's hand in mine and led us toward the diner. We easily found the right feel for our hands, fingers interlocking. I resisted the urge to swing our arms even as giddiness shot through me that I was holding my boyfriend's hand in the middle of downtown Dallas.

"You look so happy talking to the fans." Dixon looked between me and the way forward. "I love watching you go through the line. I feel like there's a teacher in you. You just light up when you're talking to a young person."

"I really enjoy hearing from them and finding out about what they got out of the performance. The student sessions we've done on the tour are awesome too. The kids are sharp with the questions they ask. I can definitely see teaching and choreographing in the future. The older I get, the more I think about that."

"How long do ballet dancers usually keep performing?"

"If I can stay mostly injury free, into my late thirties. That's fairly typical. But, man, I already ache a lot. This tour is demanding. I don't normally perform as many nights a week as we're doing here. I'm trying to take extra good care of myself, make sure I stretch really well, stay hydrated, all that stuff. Though I should probably eat better than I do." I smirked as I stole a look at Dix since some not healthy food was in our future. "How long do you think you'll keep playing?"

The sidewalk was moderately busy, although it had nothing on New York or Chicago traffic.

"Depends. There are players who go into their forties." His warm chuckle filled the air. "I don't know if I've got the stamina for that. I'm not even thirty, but some days the pain make me feel so much older. So, like you, a lot of it depends on how my body holds up."

"Par for the course in our professions." He double squeezed my hand, and the gesture sent some nice flutters through my chest. Even though I constantly touched people when I danced, the impact of one person's touch had never been as powerful as it was with Dix.

"Oh wow. Is that where we're going?" He pointed to the retro fifties-style diner a couple blocks ahead. "Everything in there has to be awesome."

"Exactly, right? As soon as Corey saw it, he proclaimed that if this wasn't some of the best food, he'd be wildly disappointed. Needless to say, he was thrilled."

Dixon held the door open as we went inside.

"Oscar, right on time. How many are we expecting tonight?" Emma always seemed to work at this time of night. She'd either greeted us or come by the table each time we'd been here.

"I think it's just us. This is my boyfriend, Dixon. He unexpectedly has an overnight stay, so I told him we had to come here."

"Table for two it is." Emma looked at Dixon as she grabbed menus from the rack on the side of the podium. "I don't think you'll be disappointed, provided you like the same kind of food the rest of these guys do." She gestured for us to follow. "Good show tonight?"

"Yes! Such a great audience tonight."

"I can't wait to see what y'all do tomorrow. I see a lot of shows there, but I've never seen this kind of show. Everyone's raving about it, so I've gotta see what all the fuss is about."

Emma, and the entire diner staff, had been awesome

to us. We'd shoved tables together and always needed the bill split. Sometimes we'd ended up signing a few programs and taking selfies with the diners too.

"That's great you're coming," I said. "We'll have to make sure we do our absolute best."

Dix sort of snorted just behind Emma and me. "Don't let him fool you. They always do their best. Tonight was the second time I've seen the show, and it just gets better. You're in for a treat. I wish I could catch it again."

"That's the best kind of review right there." Emma set the menus down as we slid into the booth. "Do you want your usual?"

"Should I order for us?" I looked to Dix.

"Of course. You trusted me with the pancakes."

"Two loaded mac and cheese, the usual water for me, and Diet Coke for him."

"We'll get that right out for you." She turned to Dix. "You'll have to let me know what you think. Tell me if it's as good as the show." She punctuated that with a wink at me.

"Oh, it's better than the show," I said right away. "There's no doubt."

She shook her head and walked away chuckling.

"Did you hear how you introduced me?"

I thought back and it hit me. A grin and blush bloomed across my face. "Oh man, it just came out. I've said it to other people but not to someone who is basically a stranger."

"It was awesome." Dix beamed at me. "I had to keep from giving you the biggest kiss right there."

"I'll take a big kiss anytime." I waggled my eyebrows. "So I'm curious. What would you want to do on a date where we're not confined by schedules?"

"I've thought about this a lot. I love to dance, but I'd be terrified to dance with you. You're the pro and I'd be the guy trying to keep up. But the thing that I really want to do—" He ran his hand over his short hair and I couldn't imagine why he seemed hesitant. "I really want to play laser tag with you again. Remember that summer that everybody had a laser tag birthday party?"

"Yes! So much laser tag. It'd be amazing to play again and see which of us survives the longest."

"So it wasn't a ridiculous idea?"

"It was great. I'd be totally into that."

"I'd also like to show you what I love in New York. Show you my favorite spot in Central Park, on the High Line. All of that. I want to see Miami with you too."

Nothing could turn me into a puddle faster than him wanting to share all the things he loved with me.

"Yes, please. We're thinking the same thing. I've already started a list of places to take you to." I pulled out my phone to show him the dozen things I already had.

Dix leaned over to look and then took my free hand in his. "Even after twenty years, we're still very much into the same things."

The server had excellent timing arriving with the food. Dix's eyes got wide at the bowl of mac and cheese placed in front of him. All talking went on hold as we indulged in the ooey, gooey goodness.

SIXTEEN

DIXON

After dinner we chattered endlessly about our obsession with various food competitions, everything from seasonal baking to chefs battling over who used mystery ingredients better. We had distinct opinions, sometimes opposing ones, about what made a good competitor. Two things we agreed on—always using fresh ingredients rather than processed and not serving under-cooked food.

When we left the diner, we walked hand in hand again. Our hands linking together as we walked seemed automatic. I liked it. I wanted it to become a thing we did.

As we neared the entrance to the hotel, I worried I'd mess things up with my next question. He'd mentioned being into a sleepover earlier, but the moment of truth was here.

"Do you want to come up?" I tripped over the words as my nerves got the better of me. "Or we can hang in the bar if you want." I added that quickly, just in case Oscar wanted more time.

"Your place, for sure." The heat in Oscar's voice surged through me. "We need some real alone time. When do you head out tomorrow? Do we get to have breakfast?"

He'd thought ahead to breakfast. Time wasn't on our side for that, though. "We might not get that. I know they want us out of here as early as possible."

"We'll make the most of tonight then. I don't have anywhere to be before the show tomorrow night, so I can sleep after you leave."

"Same for me. With the travel messed up, tomorrow's off for us."

Oscar let go of my hand and raised his arms in triumph. "No curfew!" He took my hand again and squeezed it. "I'm yours for the night."

My heart thumped hard as a flood of possibilities raced through my overactive mind. I'd be into whatever Oscar wanted to do—as much or as little.

It was a legit worry that my anticipation could get the better of me. Just the touch of our hands already had me half-hard. I struggled with wanting to take things slow, yet also wanting everything at this very moment.

As we walked through the lobby, I saw several of my teammates in the bar. Larry was there too with some of their crew. They raised a hand.

"I've got to get my key." I steered us over to their table.

"We do need that." Oscar's playful tone was perfect.

"Hey, Larry. You finally getting to relax?"

"Yeah. Everyone's settled." They sounded relieved and exhausted. Larry reached into the pocket of their team jacket and pulled out a key envelope. "You're in 923. We're headed out at six, so wake-up calls are at five thirty."

"Thanks for getting everything sorted."

They nodded. "It's been a while since we've had to organize on the fly, but we got it done. You must be Oscar. It's good to meet you. You know," Larry said, lowering their voice, "I think Dixon's the only one not upset that we're stuck here."

"It certainly made me happy." Oscar leaned into me.

"Me too." I pressed back against Oscar. "We'll leave you to it. I'm going to have the bartender put your next round on me. You all really came through today."

"You don't—"

"I know, but I'm going to." I gave Larry a look that said they wouldn't win that argument. Their crew thanked me and offered fist bumps. "Have a good night. I'll see you in the morning."

"Thanks, Dixon." Larry gave me a sleepy smile.

I nodded and headed for the bar.

"That's nice of you."

"It's the least I can do. I can't imagine what they've gone through the past few hours."

As I waited for the bartender to finish with another customer, I spotted someone who looked like Tobias sitting at the bar eating chips.

"Is that?"

Oscar sighed. "Yeah. He arrived today. He's having more talks with Corey and some local dancers too."

Tobias turned at that moment and saw Oscar. He raised his hand, made a telephone out of his thumb and pinkie finger, and mouthed *call me.*

Oscar shook his head and turned around so he was facing away. "He was never good at taking a hint."

"You want me to talk to him?" I didn't want to interfere without permission, but if Oscar wanted help discouraging Tobias, I'd do it.

"Nah. Though that would be kind of hot." Oscar rested his head on my shoulder. "I'll have an agent soon who'll do that for me."

"That's great. Nate's?"

"Yeah. I had a good meeting with Audrey and should have a contract to sign in a day or so. Then Tobias will have to go through her."

I only needed a moment with the bartender, who happily took my information. Several other players had done the same already, so she planned to split the bill between all of us. I had good teammates.

"Alright, let's get out of here."

Oscar took my hand, and this time he took the lead toward the elevator.

I caught Dimitri's eye, and he raised a glass and smiled. I gave him a nod in return. This wasn't a random hookup, but I still felt as if I'd been caught.

Talk about feeling like a teenager.

One elevator was at lobby level, so it opened immediately when Oscar tapped the button. We wasted no time getting inside, and I pushed the button for my floor.

"We could've said hello to your teammates." Oscar stepped in close. "But I'm glad we didn't." His lips grazed mine as he talked.

"No. We really couldn't have." I pressed my lips against his. "We've talked to enough people," I mumbled.

I caressed his lips with my tongue.

His firm hand cradled the back of my head, guiding our lips together in a deep and passionate kiss. As my fingers traced the contours of his back, I pulled him into a tight embrace. A whimper escaped from one of us—it could've been me, but I wasn't sure. I struggled to keep up with all the sensations. We couldn't get to the room fast enough.

The elevator stopped and dinged, and we released each other before the doors opened. I didn't care who saw us. No doubt if a security guard had been watching the elevator camera, he'd gotten a glimpse of two eager guys. But if anyone was on the other side of the door, they didn't need to see our PDA.

"Jesus. Your kisses." Oscar sounded as out of breath as I felt.

I grabbed his hand and kept a brisk pace after I figured out which way to go. I reached for the keycard in my pants pocket and fumbled it rather than unlocking the door.

"Shit," I whispered. I scrambled to get the card off the floor, which was far more difficult than it should've been.

Oscar chuckled. "It's alright." He squeezed my shoulder in the brief moment I was bent over.

Key finally in hand, I took a moment to kiss his cheek. We didn't need to rush.

I got us inside without further issue. Whoever had dropped off my luggage had left a light on, which was nice.

Oscar set his backpack next to the dresser. I took off my coat and suit jacket.

"Can I take your coat?"

"Listen to you being all formal." He slipped it off and handed it over.

"I was raised right." Keeping with the formality, I hung everything in the closet rather than laying them over a chair.

Turning from the closet, Oscar was right there—as close as he'd been in the elevator.

The low light of the room perfectly illuminated his deep brown eyes, making them sparkle. My breath caught at the sight of the handsome, sexy man before me. I couldn't decide what to do next. Option overload had set in.

Oscar moved quickly and gracefully, getting his lips back on mine.

But just a moment later, he stepped back a fraction, causing me to whimper.

"Can we get you out of these clothes?" His voice was low and seductive as he tugged my shirt out of my pants.

I could only nod.

He moved onto the buttons and quickly had the shirt

pushed off my shoulders. Goosebumps followed his light touch along my chest.

"God, you're gorgeous." He traced around my dark nipples, and I flinched at the intense pleasure. "Sorry," he chuckled as he spoke, "was that too much?"

"I'm not usually that sensitive. But you haven't touched me before either."

I'd loved the variations on his smile I'd seen during our chats. This sexy, kind of crooked smile he'd had since we'd gotten to the hotel was next level. The quirk of his mouth set the butterflies in my stomach flying and at the same time, it made me happier than I'd thought possible.

Oscar raised his arms, and I effortlessly removed his sweater. While I'd seen him perform shirtless, it hadn't prepared me for being so close to him. The sight of his flawless brown skin and tiny pert nipples caused my pants to feel uncomfortably tight.

"You like." It was more statement than question, and he gently squeezed the tent I'd sprouted.

"Very much."

He raised his eyebrows and flexed his hand around my cock. His playful forwardness captivated me. Any hesitation I'd still held about taking this step evaporated.

I pulled him in close, nuzzling my face against his neck and gently nibbling, licking, and kissing my way up to his cheek and then over to his ear. Oscar's soft hums reverberated through our embrace.

He tilted his head toward me, encouraging my kisses while his hands roamed freely across my back. Intense warmth spread from my core, igniting with every touch.

We had only just begun, yet this make-out session already surpassed anything I'd experienced before.

"These pants really have to go." Even as Oscar said it, he didn't break our embrace. "Okay?"

"Uh-hum." My agreement got lost in his mouth as he kissed me yet again.

We dropped our arms at the same time. His brown eyes blazed with lust—the pupils big and with an expression that said I was about to be dessert.

I unbuttoned and unzipped while I toed out of my shoes. He mirrored me and it became a race to get naked. Without a word, we waited for a beat and then dropped our pants and underwear together. Clothing pooled at our feet. We studied each other.

A huge smile broke across his face. I puffed out my chest a bit, relishing his look of approval.

"You're so damn hot." His tongue darted across his lower lip and I resisted going after it. "I've tried to imagine what was under the clothes." The longing sigh went right to my dick, which bounced. "It's so much more."

He stepped out of his pants and pressed into me. I ran my hand down his back and over his exposed ass and then around his hips and powerful legs. "I'd wondered if there was any padding in those tights. Damn if it's not all you. Incredible."

Oscar grinned, and it was as bright as the sun. "It's amazing how many people think there's padding. The only padding is to keep the bits protected." He cupped his cock and balls, brushing mine as he did so. I put my hand on top of his.

"You want to keep those very safe." I touched him along the side of his hand, grazing along the exposed areas of his shaft and ball sack.

He hummed. I'd found a super sensitive spot where the underside of his cock connected to his balls.

"You'd look amazing in tights. Don't think I haven't been checking out your ass in those finely tailored pants you always wear. And these legs." He caressed my thighs. "We may work out differently, but yours are just as impressive. And then there's this." He grabbed my cock. "I think you'd need an extra-large dance belt for sure."

Oscar's body was incredible. The combination of lean and muscular looked perfect and delectable. I placed my hands on his hips and effortlessly lifted him onto the dresser, which put him at a perfect height for me to get at his hardness that was begging for my attention.

SEVENTEEN

OSCAR

"Oh damn." I shuddered as Dix moved me. Did he feel it? "Nate picks me up every night, but it's nothing compared to being lifted in your strong arms."

My brain scrambled. He was touching me only at the waist, but every part of me was on fire. I didn't think I'd ever been so aroused. His gaze locked on mine as he lowered himself to my throbbing cock. Without shifting his gaze, his tongue darted along the shaft and each touch made it jump, sometimes hitting him on the nose.

I leaned back, propping myself up with my hands pressed against the dresser's top. The gentle headbutts he made against my thighs prompted me to open my legs to give him better access. I wanted his hands on me too, but that desire took a back seat to finding out what he'd do on his own.

He teased with licks from his hot, wet tongue. I couldn't control my moans, and all the while my eyes stayed locked on his.

His blissed-out face said how much he was enjoying himself. And I had the best view as he worked on my cock.

"Look what we have here." Taking my shaft between his fingers, he gently pulled back the foreskin since it stayed pretty close to the head even when I was hard. He looked between the tip, which had a bead of precum, and me as if he'd received the best present. Leaning in, he darted his tongue over the head, lapping up what was there and squeezing the shaft for more.

"Oh, Dix. Fuck." I slammed one hand into the dresser at the delicious sensation flowing from my cock. He locked his lips around the head and ran his tongue over the sensitive skin. I nearly came right then. He'd found exactly the right movement between his tongue and lips to ignite every fiber in my cock.

Somehow, though, he knew exactly when to back off.

He stood and moved me to the edge of the dresser. The powerful yet gentle movement carried so much tenderness.

I spread my legs farther to allow him to step closer. He pressed our chests together and planted an electrifying kiss on my mouth that I hungrily accepted.

We hadn't done much yet, but my brain and heart were in loud agreement that this was so right.

"My turn." I pushed off the dresser, and Dix had no choice but to step back. As soon as my feet hit the floor, I nudged him toward the bed. It was a luxurious king-sized one, and it'd be fun to use every single inch of it.

He chuckled as I gently pushed on his shoulder to

prompt him to fall back on the bed. His gorgeous, thick erection stood proudly up from a thatch of tightly curled black hair. I honestly wasn't sure how much I could take, but I'd enjoy finding out. Leaning over, I licked my lips before locking them onto his head and swirling my tongue around.

My mouth stretched with his girth. It'd been a long time since I'd sucked off anyone, and I'd never had a dick this big. My eyes watered but I persevered, sliding up and down and trying to take more each time. Dix quivered under me and nestled a hand into my curls.

"Go easy, O-man," he said even as he moaned. "It's a lot. You don't have to take it all."

I pulled off and licked my lips. "What if I want it all? And how the hell do you get this into a jock, anyway?"

Dix lifted his head and smirked at me. "It's not often I've got a raging boner when I have to tuck it away."

I slowly slipped his cock back between my lips. This time, I brought my hand into the action by caressing his balls. Dix gripped the comforter as he moaned. I slowly sucked him as my fingers wandered around and under his balls, and he rewarded me with a stream of sweet precum.

"I need you." Desire permeated Dix's voice. "Need you in my mouth. Please." The last word came out as a whimper and my cock pulsed in response.

Silently, I crawled onto the bed and maneuvered so I was over Dix. As I worked to find the right position, his hands caressed my ass.

"This is a hell of a view." Dix's breath warmed my sensitive skin with each word.

Before I got back to work on his cock, he found exactly the right spot for his tongue as he ran it over my balls and to my hole. A long, low moan rolled from me as I lapped up the precum Dix was leaking.

With my hands braced on either side of him, I was glad I could plank for minutes at a time. I plunged down on his cock, in a better position to take more. It throbbed as I explored the different contours of his shaft.

We fell into a rhythm of moaning and pleasure as we discovered all the places that turned us on. I'd never felt so many things all at once.

Dix discovered how to work my foreskin just right—nibbling, drawing it back, and paying attention to the extra-sensitive head.

Overcome by the need to kiss Dix again, I pivoted so I was lying on top of him and fixed my mouth on his. I settled myself so that his erection ran against mine and worked my hips to generate the perfect friction.

Our kisses moved between soft and easygoing to intense waves of hunger as if we might devour each other. Like everything else tonight, we quickly discovered what felt good. I held Dixon tight as the waves of pleasure reached heights I hadn't known were possible.

We never stopped kissing.

A massive shudder rolled through Dix. One of his hands shot up into my hair and the other went to my ass to increase the pressure on our cocks.

Without warning, his breath got short and the muffled sounds came in more rapid spurts.

He unloaded between us. That warmth and his extra thrusting were all it took for me to shoot. The intensity racked my body and Dix held me steady as we rode out our orgasms.

The kisses slowed, and finally I pulled back just enough to grin at Dix.

"You're incredible." I dropped a small kiss on the tip of his nose. "I've never had the feeling that I might fly apart. And yet you had me, and that was everything."

"I've never…" He looked at me, confused. "I…" He rolled his eyes and grinned. "My ability to speak is gone."

Talking didn't matter, kissing did. Even after the sensory overload, every new touch set off wild flutters in my chest.

Dix felt right in every single way.

"We should probably clean up." Dix made no move to let me go. "Or we might be stuck together forever."

"I can't remember the last time I came so much."

"Next time I'd like you in my mouth rather than across my stomach. I want to taste you."

"What about you? As much as I would have liked to try taking all that down, I might have drowned."

Laughter rumbled through him and I felt it in my chest as I lay against him. "It'd be a great mouth-to-mouth session if I had to revive you."

That set off more laughter from both of us. It would indeed be hot to be revived by him.

I rolled to my right and he let me go. "Come shower with me."

Dix rolled off the opposite side, and I happily followed him to the bathroom.

EIGHTEEN
DIXON

A LOUD RINGING jolted me awake.

I felt bad that I jumped because Oscar had been resting his head on my shoulder while draping his arm over my chest. We'd spent most of the night alternating who spooned the other, and we'd ended up like this.

Except for the wake-up call, it'd been one of the best night's sleep I'd ever had.

"I should've warned you how loud the phones are," Oscar mumbled.

It rang again. Another phone rang on the other side of the wall too. I reached for the bedside table, but the phone wasn't there.

Oscar moved, and in the darkness I could make out him reaching for the other table. He answered it mid-ring and hung up.

Meanwhile, the one next door was still ringing.

"I usually set my alarm five minutes before the wake-up calls so I can ease into being awake before the phone gets me." Rolling onto my side, I found Oscar in the same position. "Hotel phones are never nice this time of morning."

"That's a brilliant idea. I'm going to do that. There's always a couple of days in each city we've got to be up early for something."

I moved closer and wrapped my arm around him, drawing us close. Oscar's skin was warm against me, and I knew right here was the most comfortable place I could be. Our lips met gently, and we shared a perfect wake-up kiss. I'd thought sleeping next to him was perfect, but waking up in the same bed was pretty perfect too.

"Thanks for the great night," I said between kisses.

"Hmmm. Thank you."

Before I could react, he rolled me onto my back and moved on top of me. He peppered my face and neck with kisses.

"I shouldn't be doing this since you have to go, but I want to burn all of this into my memory since it'll be a while before it happens again."

He kept going down my chest. His growing erection pressed into me, which triggered mine. All this when I probably had twenty minutes before I needed to be in the lobby.

A noise escaped him, a mixture of moan and growl, as he gave me a heated glare.

He slid his way down to my cock and yanked at my underwear.

"We don't—"

He swallowed my shaft down and hungrily worked

his tongue over it. This was different, more urgent than what he'd done last night. He didn't even wait to get my boxers fully off, just held the waistband down to get what he wanted.

His lips were tight around my hard-on and his tongue seemed to be everywhere at the same time.

"Fuck, O-man."

My body quivered as I lay on the bed, completely at the mercy of Oscar's skilled mouth. His every movement sent shockwaves of pleasure through me. I surrendered myself to him, not caring if I was latc.

How he managed to be so focused and keep his mouth locked on me, I didn't know.

Each time my cock head hit the back of his throat, the sensations reached another level. Sometimes he didn't let it go that deep, but others he'd let it happen repeatedly.

I struggled to keep my moans from getting too loud as he kept going. He didn't even hesitate when my hips bucked and sent my cock deeper than it had ever been.

"Fuck, fuck, fuck."

Oscar responded to that by burying his nose against my pubes. My dick went again to that deep spot and this time he kept it there, working his throat, lips, tongue, all of it.

I'd never quaked so hard.

"I'm gonna... gonna come."

He didn't back off. Instead, he returned to sliding up and down my shaft, taking me deep each time.

I grabbed at whatever bits of the sheets I could to hold on to as I unloaded, and Oscar stayed on me as shot after shot flowed. As the orgasm eased, he slowed down his sucking.

"Oh my God. That was incredible," I said when he released my cock.

He held on to my softening dick and licked the head one last time.

"There. Now you're all cleaned up and ready to travel." Gently, he arranged my cock in my boxers and smoothed them out.

"You think I'm able to stand after that?" My voice was soft as I swam in the afterglow of my release.

Oscar came back up and nestled against my side. I turned and kissed him deeply.

"That was fun." He sounded pleased with himself. "I'm definitely doing that again sometime."

"Anytime you want. You didn't give away last night how talented you are in that area."

"I'm glad I could take all of you." He gave me a quick kiss. "Now, we gotta get you going. I don't want your teammates mad at me for making everyone late."

"Fine. If you insist." I gave him my best frustrated voice.

We got up and hurried around the room, hastily getting dressed. I wore the same clothes I'd gone to the show in to save the time of getting something out of my bag.

"This was probably the best first date ever."

"I agree," he said, grabbing his backpack from where he'd dropped it.

I grabbed my roller bag and backpack and we headed out.

The looks from some of the team were priceless as Oscar came down to the lobby with me as we gathered to board the bus to the airport. While most of them knew he and I had gotten together last night, it said even more that he'd come down to see me off.

We shared a scorching kiss before I walked out of the hotel. Thankfully, no one who saw it said anything to draw more attention to us.

Oscar actually stood at the windows and watched the bus pull out.

As I watched him wave goodbye, I understood the true meaning of heartache. The time when we could spend an entire day together couldn't get here soon enough.

We hadn't even gotten on the freeway when my phone buzzed.

Oscar: Miss you already! Talk to you this afternoon.

A brown heart and a black heart followed the message.

Dixon: I wish I could make them turn this bus around!

I added the hearts too, but reversed them.

The ride to the airport was quiet, as it always was when we traveled super early. I hunched into the seat and closed my eyes. While the couple hours of sleep I'd had last night had been fantastic, I'd had a few moments where I'd simply lain in that nice half-asleep, half-awake zone enjoying him beside me.

At the airport, Caleb stepped in next to me as we boarded the plane. "Good night?"

I brought my hand to my heart as I smiled. "Very."

He clapped me on the shoulder and pulled me into a sideways hug. "Good for you."

"It's like all the talking—the texts, phone calls, when we met up—let us take that leap. The hard part begins now, trying to date someone who lives far away. Oscar wants it too. We just have to figure out what that means."

In a repeat of a few weeks ago, Caleb and I ended up in the same seats so we could talk before takeoff. This time Dimitri didn't look confused about Caleb taking the extra moments with me.

"I hope you're able to find what works. You know Aaron and I are only a couple hours' drive apart, but there are other guys in the league who are separated by hundreds or thousands of miles."

I'd recently Googled that. It happened in all the pro sports and it inspired me to know that people made it work. "Is it insane that I've already considered getting a place in Miami for the off season?"

Caleb shook his head and chuckled. "Nope. I'd say you're a man who's in love and looking for a way to be near his man as often as possible."

I closed my mouth before the next question came out. I'd only known Caleb for about six months, and I didn't want to pry. His cocked eyebrow goaded me into continuing.

"How did your parents take it when you reconnected with Aaron?"

"Thrilled doesn't fully describe it. They didn't know about the crushes we'd had on each other, but they were happy when we told them." When I said nothing after a few moments, he asked exactly what I was thinking about. "Are your parents going to be cool?"

"Think so. I told mine I'd found Oscar at the show that night and they thought it was great we connected. They don't know any more, though. And I've always loved Oscar's folks. He's had the same guess-who-I-found discussion. Maybe we should just get them all on the phone at the same time and tell them."

"That's either the best idea or the worst."

I hummed in response.

"Unfortunately, you probably won't know which until it's happening."

I quickly covered my mouth so I didn't yawn in his face.

"You should settle in." Caleb stood just as the safety announcement started, but he leaned back so I could hear him over the flight attendant. "I was serious when I said we should all get together, so let me know when he's in New York again. I'd love to get to know him. We can talk about the long distance thing too... or not. Either way, it'd be great to hang out."

"Thanks. That'd be cool."

We exchanged a fist bump, and he went across the

aisle and dropped into the seat next to Dimitri. They chatted as the engine got louder and the safety announcements droned on.

I loved Caleb. I'd always had great captains, but he had something special. He always had confidence in the team and seemed to know what to say to get our best. He'd even managed to get us as tight on the ice as off. Any team I'd been part of had some personalities that didn't quite mesh. Here, though, we had a great camaraderie and I thought a lot of that was Caleb.

I popped in my AirPods and set my phone to play random tunes. As I drifted off, flashes of last night and this morning played in my head.

NINETEEN

OSCAR

I DIDN'T CARE if I looked like a lovesick puppy as I stayed at the window, watching until the team bus disappeared around the corner.

Last night had exceeded even the wildest expectations I'd had about what it would be like to be with Dix. The sex had been sensual, erotic, and a perfect mix of gentle and wild that had left me completely fulfilled.

Sleeping with him had been simply incredible. It'd never occurred to me how comforting it could be to lie against someone who meant the world to you. Even though we'd only actually slept a few hours, it had been the best rest I'd ever had.

Part of me regretted that we hadn't talked more. There were so many things to figure out.

What I was sure of as I stood at the window was that I absolutely loved Dixon Cliff.

I pulled my phone out and before I could second-guess sending a text, especially since we'd just said good-bye, I typed a message.

Oscar: Miss you already! Talk to you this afternoon.

I added two hearts—a brown one and a black one—to punctuate the message.

I headed for the elevators. Sometimes it sucked to be an adult. Part of me wanted to go to the airport and catch a plane to meet him in New York when he landed. Thankfully, my rational side knew that while figuring out our relationship wouldn't be easy, it was also going to be the best thing ever.

My phone buzzed in my hand.

Dixon: I wish I could make them turn this bus around!

I stared at the screen and at the hearts he'd added.

Despite not feeling sleepy, I *needed* sleep. Hopefully, closing my eyes and Nate's serene nature sounds would help me drift off easily. I didn't know how I was supposed to find a comfortable position, though, after experiencing sleeping with Dix by my side.

As I passed the front desk, the person working there said good morning, and I said it back and smiled. It was probably the goofiest smile because I was off-the-charts happy. It was too bad I didn't have a TV thing this morning to capitalize on this mood.

"Is he why you haven't gotten back to me?" Tobias's

voice stopped me mid-stride and wiped the smile off my face. "He was in Denver with you and now he's here too. A hockey player, really?"

I steeled myself to deal with him before I turned in his direction. "I haven't called you because I have nothing to say." It was a struggle to keep the annoyance out of my voice. "I told you I wasn't interested in joining your company."

"Come on, Oscar. You've grown so much as a dancer. This is a chance to be a founding member in something new." He checked his phone before standing and coming over to me with his luggage in tow. "I can help you be even better."

It was too early for this.

"You still don't understand no when you hear it, do you? Let me be clearer. I don't want to work with you." Each word carried extra emphasis to drive my point into his mind.

I pivoted, determined to get to the elevators. He grabbed my arm before I could even go a step.

"What did you tell your castmates?" Frustration and anger crept into his tone. "None of them will join. Corey seemed like a lock, but last night he declined."

"There's enough stuff about you online from your time in Miami that I didn't need to say anything. It's easy to find out what you're like to work with. From what little I've seen of you, I don't think you've changed much."

He shot daggers at me with his eyes.

"Look—" His phone vibrated in his hand, and he

stole a look at the screen. "My car's here. We'll finish this later." Tobias turned and headed for the door.

"No, we won't. It's already done."

He stopped and looked back but decided not to say anything else.

I didn't give him the chance to reconsider and hurried to the safety of the elevators. With everyone saying no, maybe that meant he wouldn't turn up in another city.

At the door to my room, I held my phone over the door sensor. The lock click was so loud I flinched.

Why was everything so loud here?

Nate had a high tolerance for sound, so fingers crossed he'd slept through that.

Another bonus to rooming with Nate was that he also liked leaving the bathroom light on so we could find our way in the dark. I had just enough light through the slightly ajar door not to bump around the room.

I dropped my backpack by the dresser, triggering flashbacks of what Dix and I had done a few hours ago. I toed off my shoes and stripped down to my underwear, leaving my clothes in a heap on the floor.

"It's about time you got home."

I squeaked at Nate's voice. "Sorry. I tried to be quiet."

In the dim light, Nate's silhouette was visible as he rolled over and propped his head up on his hand. "Coming in at this hour must mean everything was good." He studied me more. "Or was it? Why do you look annoyed?"

"The night was the best." I lay down on my bed and faced Nate in a similar position to his. "I'm annoyed because while I was downstairs saying goodbye to Dix, I ran into Tobias."

"Oh God. I'm sorry. Do we need to talk about that, or can we focus on your night?"

"My night, for sure." My smile was back. "Tobias isn't worth more time."

"Yay." Nate's enthusiasm brought my happiness right back to the surface. "You know, the longer you were gone, the more certain I was it was all good. I felt a little weird, though, like I was a parent waiting for their kid to come home. Todd laughed at me when I told him I hoped the door wasn't gonna open before I fell asleep."

"If I'm honest, I feel like a teenager in a cheesy movie where I'll end up pining for my love because we're separated. Which is crazy since we've just ended a twenty-year separation."

"If you decide you need to break into a chorus of 'Summer Nights,' I'll fall in line as backup."

I snort laughed. Nate had a way of saying the most hilarious things, usually with a good musical reference. "Is it insane that I want to tell Dix I love him, even with all the distance between us? I mean, seriously, what are the odds that we're ever going to be in the same city for more than a minute? He can't just switch teams—at least I don't think he can. It's not the easiest thing to switch companies either. Plus we both like where we are professionally right now."

"When Todd and I decided to go for it, we didn't know how it was going to work. I had the *American Next Top Dancer* tour and then a Broadway gig. He had his job with the production company. We racked up a ton of airline miles. I'd go to LA during tour breaks or he'd come see me when he had time off. We hadn't been in the same place for nearly eighteen months when he got his gig at The Met. If you two want it, you can definitely make it work."

"You sound like a love guru or something." I thought for a moment. "You're right, though. Life keeps people separated sometimes—especially in showbiz and sports. Oh man. I wish I'd said 'I love you' before he got on the bus. Just so he'd know."

"Tell him the next time you talk. I'm guessing that'll be later today."

"Of course."

"There you go. And please don't be one of the people who goes back and forth on should you say it first or should you do it on the phone or in person. If it's in your heart, just say it."

I definitely loved him. Fear had held me back from saying it this morning. But I was ready. If he wasn't, he could say so and I'd understand.

"Again with the good advice. Maybe you should have a podcast or something. Help people sort out what to do."

Nate laughed as he rolled onto his back. "Can you imagine? I'm happy just helping friends out when I can. Now, let's get some sleep. We'll talk more over breakfast —or maybe we'll call it brunch."

"Brunch and advice from the love guru. I like it."

A pillow smashed into my face, followed by a giggle from the next bed. I tossed it back, and he caught it before it hit him. Even when Nate was sleepy, his reflexes were on point.

"Talk to you in a few hours." I dropped my head to my pillow as Nate replied with only a "mmm-hmmm."

I snuggled into the covers but missed Dix at my side.

TWENTY

DIXON

My feelings were jumbled as I waited to talk to Oscar in a few hours. I couldn't tell if it was nervousness or excitement, but my emotions were all over the place.

Thankfully, with the lack of sleep last night, I'd conked out on the plane, so I'd had those couple of hours when I couldn't overthink things.

Once I was awake, though, I fixated on how to say "I love you" for the first time, on the phone, without sounding ridiculous.

The question bouncing around my mind after that was, what if he wasn't ready to hear those words?

For me, the overnight in Dallas had solidified what I'd known for a while.

The future I wanted had Oscar and me together.

It had to be said. There was no reason to put it off further.

Once I got home, I threw myself into things around the apartment. The recent road trip had left me with a few loads of laundry to do as well as a stack of mail to go through. Plus we were about to kick off a home stint. With a couple of weeks at home, my fridge needed more than a pitcher of water, some shredded cheese, and a few condiments.

I'd texted Oscar a hello on the bus ride to the practice facility where our cars were. It took a while for him to respond because he'd gone with Alexi and some of the other dancers to visit a youth group that Alexi worked with in the city.

Our texts were simple, but I enjoyed the small talk. These chats connected us and let us randomly share things about our days. It sounded like he'd had a great time teaching some basic dance moves to some thirteen- and fourteen-year-olds.

Our evening "date" would come around five. We planned to chat during the time he ate his light preshow dinner.

I debated between saying the words over dinner or waiting until after his performance. I didn't know which option was better. If I upset him, I didn't want him to carry that into his dancing. At the same time, I didn't want to disrupt another night's sleep.

No way could I wait until we were in person next. We didn't even know when that would be yet. He still had two weeks on the road and I didn't overlap with him again.

After I'd done everything I could do to distract myself in the apartment, I threw on some sweats and headed out for a jog along the Hudson. One of my favorite parts of living downtown was being so close to the river and the running and cycling paths. It was a perfect day with the sun out and mild temperatures, a pleasant surprise after the weather that had kept us in Dallas yesterday.

I'd gone a dozen blocks when Siri interrupted the tunes. "Incoming call. Oscar."

He was a couple of hours early.

I double tapped my AirPod. "Hey! This is a pleasant surprise."

I exited the running path and headed over to one of the many benches along the riverfront.

"You know, I decided I didn't have to wait to talk to you. I could ring you up while I was having some tea. Texting is nice, but hearing your voice is always better."

As I dropped onto the bench, I pulled my phone from my hoodie pocket and switched over to video FaceTime so we could see each other.

He looked stunning as always. His curly brown hair, styled just so with a perfect fade at the sides. The beautiful light brown eyes staring back at me. The only problem was I really wanted to kiss those luscious full lips.

"I was just out for a run. With the gorgeous day, I thought I'd take advantage."

"Look at you all sexy with that blue sky behind you. Wish I was there to enjoy it with you."

"That'd be awesome. I don't think you knew when I pointed out where I lived, but the river is only a few blocks away. This is one of my favorite places that I will bring you for a walk, a picnic, a snowball fight, or all three."

His eyes got a little extra spark in them and his lips curled into a smile I'd begun to recognize as mine. He smiled a lot, but he seemed to have one that was just for me. It made me warm and tingly every time he flashed it.

"Yes, please. It's a lot of effort to get to the water in Miami. I mean, we're surrounded by it, but the beaches are usually so packed."

"It can get overcrowded here too. But I also know the best times when it's chill, like afternoons in the middle of the week or early morning as the sun comes up."

Oscar chuckled, which also made my heart soar. "That sounds perfect for two guys who often work weekends and nights."

"Exactly." All right, it was time to seize the moment. "I had an amazing night last night, O-man. I've never been so thankful for a flight delay." My mouth turned into a desert, but I had to get this out. "I wish I'd said this before I left, but you need to know that I really want a relationship with you. If you're into it, I'd really like to give it a go."

I was grateful we were talking on FaceTime. I couldn't imagine saying this without being able to see his reaction. His smile grew bigger than I'd ever seen it.

"Oscar, I love you."

"Dix, I love you."

No way.

Had that just happened? We said it at the same time.

I sat there in shock and pure happiness. My video

image in the top corner displayed my mouth hanging open in disbelief.

Oscar was the same.

"I can't believe we did that," he said. "If that's not a sign, I don't know what is. Just in case you didn't hear it clearly, let me say it again. I love you."

"You better believe I heard it. And I want us to say it to each other all the time. I love you. So much."

I let out a yelp of joy and fist pumped to the sky in triumph. This was better than a game-winning goal. I'd just scored the best guy.

A few people sitting on other benches or walking along the path glanced over at me to see what the fuss was about. The best reaction came from Oscar, though. He shook his head and hid his face in his hand.

The day could not get better—spending the night with him and confirming how we felt.

TWENTY-ONE
OSCAR

"Oscar, I love you."

"Dix, I love you."

My heart beat double time as we spoke simultaneously. I could barely contain the overwhelming joy coursing through me.

His expression was priceless. A mix of surprise and happiness came from the other side of the screen.

"I can't believe we did that." Had I ever been this happy? I could barely contain myself as I sat in an oversized comfy chair at the cafe around the corner from the hotel. "If that's not a sign, I don't know what is. Just in case you didn't hear it clearly, let me say it again. I love you."

"You better believe I heard it. And I want us to say it to each other all the time. I love you. So much."

Dixon's yelp and fist pump punctuated the moment perfectly. I shook my head and his my face in my hand, slightly overwhelmed by what we'd done.

We each wanted this as much as the other. My fear dissipated, as neither of us had shown any hesitation.

"The only thing that would have made this better would have been to do it in person. But I'm crazy happy it's out there. I've been trying to figure out the right way to tell you."

"Let's just say that my apartment is cleaner and more organized than it usually is. I finally went out for a run because I'd run out of things to do. It's like pregame jitters amped to eleven."

Incredible. Dix and I had been on the same page this entire time, including not knowing how to actually say the words.

"Can we promise to say whatever is on our minds in the future? No more trying to find the right time, or the right words?"

Again, Dix didn't have to think it over. "Absolutely. It'll be so much easier than walking on eggshells around each other."

He looked so damn happy. The sunny day did make his eyes sparkle, even through the phone screen. A chuckle escaped me, thinking about how I didn't usually see him in the daytime.

"What?"

"It's silly. I just realized that we've spent practically no time together during the day. We might as well be vampires. Anyway, you look incredible."

"I'll have to take some selfies while I'm out here so you can see me in a natural environment." Dix moved the phone so I could see more of his surroundings, putting his long arms to good use.

"I look forward to the summer view. Maybe you in a pair of shorts. Sweat glistening on your chest. Maybe I could take the pictures so I have a good, curated collection for when we're in different cities."

Dix's mouth dropped open. He couldn't fool me, though. No way had that surprised him.

"Oscar Salazar! I don't even know what to say."

I raised my eyebrow, letting him know I didn't believe his outburst.

"If we're taking pictures like that, then I get some of you too. I imagine you look stunning in the summer sun."

"Deal. We've got a photo shoot to plan as soon as the weather warms up."

We had matching smirks, as if we had both just won something.

I stared intensely at Dixon, taking in every nuance of him. I hadn't known it was possible to have a comfortable silence across FaceTime, but that was what this was.

"I want to figure out our schedules and when we can be together again. We should have a proper celebration of this new phase of us."

Planning had never sounded so good. "For sure. Let's sort out the summer. And even before that, if you're up for it, let's always try to have a meal together. That way we'd always make sure we had time to talk."

"And before bed too, as often as possible. If we can't be in the same actual place, we can make sure we're together virtually."

"I love it." The phone shook in my hand with the euphoria rushing through me. "Honest answer on this, is it too soon to tell our parents?"

"No, it's not." Had Dix thought about it already? He didn't even pause for a thought. "I don't think we need to hide that we're boyfriends. Let's figure that out? It'd be outstanding to get us all together rather tell them over the phone."

"This is one of the reasons we're going to be a great couple. We seem to have the same thoughts."

"Of course we do." Dix shot me another huge smile. "I think our parents will be happy but concerned that we're not actually in the same place. We'll show them what's possible, though."

"Yes, we will!"

I wondered how my traditional parents would handle the long distance concept. They'd never been apart more than a few days in the years they'd been together.

A text message alert dropped over the top part of my screen. It was from the artistic director at Miami City Ballet.

Tiana: Oscar, sorry to reach out while you're on tour. Can you please call me when you get a chance? Tobias Clark is causing trouble, and you need to know what's going on.

I groaned and dismissed the alert.

"What's wrong? I've never seen you frown like that."

"Something's up with Tobias. I got a text from Miami

and they asked me to call. How does he just keep popping up?" Sighing, I ran a hand through my hair. "I ran into him after we said goodbye. He was leaving and all annoyed that no one from the cast wanted to join his company."

"What a jerk."

"I can think of stronger words than 'jerk' for him. He even tried to blame you for me not signing up with him."

Dix looked skyward and shook his head. "As if I would block you from doing something you wanted to do." Dix looked back at the screen. "I'm sorry he won't just go away."

"I suppose I should find out what's going on." I hated ending our chat on a downer, but things couldn't always be perfect.

"And I should get moving. It's a little chilly to sit still for too long. Do you still want to have dinner before the show, or should we chat after?"

"Why not both? What better way to counteract whatever Tobias stirred up than talking with my man?"

"Both it is!" Dix's excitement never got old, and I was certain it never would. "I'll talk to you in a couple of hours then."

"Enjoy the rest of the run," I said. "Love you."

"I love you too." Dixon kissed at the screen and I did the same.

He disconnected and I stared at the blank screen, head over heels in love but not excited about the call I had to make next.

TWENTY-TWO

DIXON

Today was apparently random text day.

After I got cleaned up from the run, I had a message from Sheri, who was in the team's PR department, asking me to call her. If Oscar hadn't gotten the message from Miami, I wouldn't have thought anything of it, but the timing made me wonder about the coincidence.

"Dixon, thanks for getting back to me so quickly." She didn't sound stressed, so that was good. "Sorry to bother you on your day off, especially after the travel problems."

"Not a problem. It's always good to hear from you." And that was true. She knew I'd do whatever PR wanted, and Sheri was always good to work with.

"A couple of odd things came into my inbox today. Two reporters, from different outlets, sent me a picture of you and Oscar that was shot in the hotel's lobby this morning."

Shit.

"I have a pretty good idea where it came from."

"Oh? I hadn't expected that. The message came from an address that was clearly trying to be anonymous. It was vague and passive aggressive too, saying, 'Thought you might want to look into what Dixon Cliff is up to.' It honestly made me laugh at how amateur gossipy it is."

"Oscar's ex isn't too happy with him at the moment for professional reasons. Oscar actually had a run-in with him this morning after we left. He didn't mention anything about a picture, but I can imagine this guy being behind it. How much of a problem is this?"

"From the team perspective, none. I wanted to let you know it's circulating. The reporters who sent it to me aren't doing anything with it because it doesn't matter. They wanted me to have a heads-up since it's clearly someone looking to cause trouble. If you need help with it for any reason, we're here for you."

I loved the team so much. Even though this had nothing to do with team operations, they were still willing to help.

Oscar and I hadn't snapped any selfies together yet, so I couldn't just post one of my own to get ahead of any posts announcing that we were a couple.

I hated that this might be how my family found out. They would never let me forget they'd had to hear about a relationship from anyone other than me.

"Can you send me the picture? I'd like to let Oscar know this is happening. Also, could we use the picture if you send it to us? Maybe post it ahead of anyone else?"

"It's on the way to you. I don't recommend posting

the original since whoever shot it didn't send it to you directly. If it's posted somewhere else, then it's open season and you can comment or repost all you want. What were you thinking?"

I thought for a moment before I spoke. "If we posted just to announce we're boyfriends, that would be great. I imagine that if we had a picture we'd shot, we'd try to get ahead of that picture with a short message. We're just barely to the stage where we'd consider doing that. It's one thing if it was a fan who saw that and posted it, but if it's Oscar's ex like I think it is, that's different."

"Mmmm," was all that Sheri offered.

"Anyway, sorry you ended up having to spend time on it."

"It's really not a problem." Her tone made me more confident that was true. "I wish I had some brilliant idea for you. What I can do is let you know if this ends up posted. We're always on the lookout for players getting mentioned in articles or social media, so we'll know if it's online. I'll add Oscar's name to our watch list too, to increase chances of finding it."

"You don't have to do that." I really didn't want it to become a thing.

"We need to do it anyway with you two becoming more serious. We monitor for spouses, significant others, and sometimes kids and extended family, just in case anything bubbles up that might be a concern. It's part of keeping the team and everyone closely associated with it safe."

This was news to me and another great example of

being looked out for. Caleb had an assistant I'd met, and I knew he managed Caleb's social media among other things. It had never occurred to me that the team had a process to watch for stories and posts.

"Thanks for doing that. I appreciate it. I'll let you know if I find out anything else going on. Oscar had a call from his ballet company earlier related to his ex. Sounds like it might be something."

"I'm so sorry you two are dealing with this. I'm serious. If you need anything, just let me know. You don't have to deal with the press or social media alone."

"I appreciate that."

"Alright, I'll let you get back to your day off."

"Thanks, Sheri. Have a good one."

I disconnected and swiped over to my inbox. Sheri's email was at the top, so I opened it and tapped on the image icon.

In the dim lighting, the picture was centered on Oscar and me. It was easy to see that it was us, even with our faces slightly obscured. The image captured us at an angle, with more of Oscar's face visible while only a small portion of mine showed. Our embrace and kiss were captured perfectly.

Truth be told, the picture was great. I wish it had come to me under better circumstances.

What a day—from waking up next to Oscar, to a wonderful goodbye, and then everything we'd said over the phone. The trouble with Tobias changed nothing about how I felt about Oscar. My only concern was that our parents would find out from some stupid story rather than us.

The plan of getting everyone together as a reunion of the families and to share our news had been a perfect idea but, thanks to Tobias, it seemed less likely that we'd be able to pull that off. There was nothing wrong, though, about telling them on the phone and then celebrating when we could all be together.

I shot a text to Oscar. We were going to talk in a couple hours anyway, but if he was free now, I wanted to tell him about the picture. Knowing what happened in Miami would also be good.

Dixon: Any chance you're free to talk? Besides what's happening in Miami, Tobias has been busy with contacts the team has too. I sent you an email you'll want to see.

"A LAWSUIT? Seriously? For something that happened so long ago?" I struggled to use my indoor voice because what Tiana had shared was unbelievable.

"We're all stunned too, although maybe we shouldn't be." Tiana had been a choreographer when I'd been in school and a couple of years ago she'd risen to the artistic director position. She was wonderful to work with and was very familiar with Tobias and his behavior. "He's tried to recruit several dancers here and from what I've heard, everyone rejected him. I'm not sure why he would try to approach people here, given his history."

"How is it he can suddenly sue for this now?"

"From what I gather, it's not the specific incidents that occurred but rather his belief that the company, and certain individuals, are discussing it and that's discouraging others from working with him. He insists it's negatively affecting his business. Basically, he's unhappy that his reputation has caught up with him."

"Unbelievable. And let me guess, I'm on the list of *certain individuals?*"

"I'm afraid so. He's named everyone who ever complained about him."

At least I was in good company since he'd had more than a dozen complaints lodged against him.

"What do I need to do?"

"For the current company members involved, Bart can handle the defense if you want him to. You're also welcome to hire your own attorney. Whatever you're the most comfortable with."

"I'm happy for Bart to handle it."

I trusted him to deal with Tobias. Bart had been the attorney for the company when all of this had gone down and he'd been great.

"He'll send you something to sign to make it official. We're looking at how to make it go away as quickly as possible while making it clear no one here is to blame."

"I appreciate that."

Leave it to Tobias to stir something up on what should be a super happy, awesome day with everything Dix and I had said to each other.

"In the meantime, if Tobias approaches, please tell him to direct all communication to Bart."

"Will do. Hopefully, I won't have to. I told him this morning to leave me alone."

"Oh, you saw him today?"

"Yeah. I happened to see him as he was leaving the hotel. We had a few words."

"Can you please send an email to Bart and let him know what was said?"

"Of course."

"Thanks, Oscar. I need to let you go so I can make more calls about this."

"Okay, Tiana. Let me know if you need anything."

"Will do. Have a good show tonight."

"Thanks. Bye."

I ended the call and let go the sigh I'd kept in. The situation was a complete mess. I couldn't imagine Audrey being thrilled about having a new client named in a lawsuit.

The phone screen lit up with a text from Dixon.

What could Tobias possibly do to his team?

I swiped over to my inbox, opened Dix's email, and skimmed the details. What on earth was this?

I tapped to open the image. It was Dix and me from this morning.

"What a jerk," I said as the door to the room opened. Nate came in in shorts and a T-shirt. His hair was damp and sticking up at odd angles like it always did after a swim.

"Who's a jerk?"

"One guess." I handed Nate my phone with the picture still on screen.

"Awww. Cute picture. Wait, Dixon isn't the jerk, I hope." He handed the phone back, looking confused.

"Oh no. Dix is never a jerk. Tobias took that picture this morning and is sending it around. He's also decided to sue some people, including me."

"Holy shit. Are you okay? Do you need a lawyer? We can call Audrey right now." Nate spread his towel on his bed and sat down with a serious look I wasn't used to seeing off stage.

His seriousness helped calm down my desire to hunt Tobias down and wring his neck. I appreciated how he wanted immediately to help.

"I'm fine." I shrugged, not knowing what else to do. "Just more pissed off than I've been in a long time."

"How's Dixon taking all the drama?"

"I don't know yet. He sent me the picture while I was finding out about the suit. He asked me to call."

"You should do that." Nate popped up and took the towel with him. "I'm going to shower off the chlorine and give you some privacy."

"Thanks."

As he closed the door, I tapped Dix's name on the text message to FaceTime him.

"Hey!" He picked up the call immediately, as if his finger had been hovering over the screen, ready to answer. He sounded upbeat and was smiling, which I took as a good sign. "How are you doing? I imagine that picture only added to the problems you had to talk to Miami about."

I couldn't suppress a chuckle. The situation was so ridiculous that laughing seemed the best thing to do. "I don't think they've seen it. Tobias is suing Miami City Ballet, and me, and some others too. Claims we're keeping him from starting his company."

"That little shit. Are you okay? Is there anything I can do?"

"I'm okay. Somewhere between stunned, angry, and amused. I wish I could say I was surprised, but this kind of fits Tobias, although it's next level. So what's going on with the picture exactly?"

As Dix laid out the story, my mouth dropped open. The effort Tobias was going to for some kind of revenge was incredible.

"I'm glad your team handled it okay. And it's nice to know that not all journalists are interested in that gossip stuff either."

"What would you think of posting on our socials that we're boyfriends? We'd be ahead of anyone who decided to use the picture."

I nodded even as I thought about that. "It makes sense. There's nothing to hide, and I'd rather be the one to share the news about my amazing boyfriend than let someone else do it."

The telltale sound of a screenshot being captured came through the phone.

"What did you just do?"

"Snapped a picture of us talking. It's the closest thing to a picture of us together."

"I hope I don't look goofy."

"Not at all. You're super cute and handsome as always."

I snapped my own screenshot because it was a good idea. "There. Now I've got one too. We'll be all matchy-matchy."

"Perfect. Next time we're together, we'll have to take some real selfies."

"For sure. But don't think that'll take the place of the summer photo shoot."

"It won't. Not at all. I'm looking forward to that shoot." Dix's expression held a glint of mischief, leaving me curious about what he had planned for the photo shoot. Summer needed to get here faster.

"I'm going to call my parents tonight and tell them about us. I don't think we can wait to get everyone together."

"Yeah. I'll do that too. My parents aren't on social media too much, but you never know."

"My mom follows hockey social media way too much. She might already sense there's a picture out there she hasn't seen yet."

I snorted because that was too funny and snorted again before I could control myself. "I knew your mom was many things, but I didn't realize that she was some kind of social media Jedi."

That made him crack up even if he didn't snort. I'd have to figure out what would get that out of him.

We probably wouldn't get through every difficulty thrown at us as easily as we'd navigated this one so far. Hopefully we'd always do it with this much love and calmness.

"We should still get everyone together. A sort of family reunion."

"For sure!" Dix shifted to a more serious expression.

"So, do you need a lawyer or something? We didn't really finish talking about that lawsuit thing."

"The company's lawyer can handle it, so that'll be pretty easy. I need to let my agent know, and tour management. Hopefully, that won't cause any issues. What a pain in the ass all of this is."

I let out a heavy sigh and raked my fingers through my curls, temporarily losing the humor about the situation that I'd had earlier.

"I wish I was there to support you," Dix said softly.

"I'm okay, though."

"I know. Still, give you a hug, a kiss, be there instead of on a screen."

"But you're here and we're talking. Sometimes that's all it can be. Believe me, I know you've got my back."

"And I know you've got mine. I love you, O-man."

Those words had my heart bursting with joy. "Love you too." I stole a look at the time. "I need to make some more calls, and I've got a cute picture to post before we have dinner."

Dix nodded. "I look forward to that. Hopefully, we won't have to say Tobias's name for at least the rest of the day."

"Please, yes." I managed a laugh at that.

"Talk to you soon. Love you."

"See you then." I blew him a kiss and disconnected the call.

While I had calls to make, I was more interested in trying to figure out exactly what I wanted to post about my boyfriend.

TWENTY-FOUR

MESSAGES FROM THE ROAD

Oscar: Guess what?

Dixon: You're the best boyfriend ever?

Oscar: Awww. Thank you. But that's not it. Guess again?

Dixon: What's the category? Otherwise I'm going to give the same answer again.

Oscar: What's the best news I could have?

Dixon: You're coming to dance with a company in New York?

Oscar: Okay, that would be pretty great. But that's not it either.

Dixon: I've got too many options for the best news. Tell me, please. The suspense is killing me.

Oscar: Tobias is dropping the suit. Apparently, his producing partner isn't thrilled since the suit is probably a bigger problem than the number of people Tobias didn't recruit so far.

Dixon: Sounds like karma to me.

Oscar: Yup. And it took less than a week to bite him. I'd been prepared for it to drag on for months. Now it's all done and I'm not even back in Miami yet.

Dixon: I'm glad you don't have to drag that into the summer.

Oscar: Me too. I'm glad we're not doing anything about the picture either.

Dixon: Yeah. All the responses I've gotten to it since it hit were what I'd expected. Most people are happy for us, and the haters are just the haters.

Oscar: I'm happy to just block those people if I find them.

Dixon: Oh, I finally signed a picture printout last night in Vegas.

Oscar: It's about time. I've been signing them for days now. I'm glad someone finally got you to sign something besides a jersey or a puck.

Dixon: LOL. It'd be cool if someone had me sign one you'd already signed.

Oscar: Oh yeah! Or even better if we somehow signed one at the same time.

Dixon: Is it weird we're talking about autograph scenarios?

Oscar: Probably. What are you up to anyway? I suppose I should've asked that before I just started chatting away.

Dixon: You're good. I'm waiting for a team meeting to start.

Oscar: It's nice when we're in the same time zone. Makes it so easy to talk. But being in the same state and not being able to see you isn't fair.

Dixon: I know. I wish there was an easy, reliable way to get from San Jose to San Diego.

Oscar: Can you imagine? Making the trip and then not getting back on time because of flight delays. I think the tour manager would restrain me if I even considered trying.

Dixon: Oh, completely. Just asking the question would get a what-are-you-thinking look from Coach.

Oscar: Only twelve days until the tour's over and then no more hopping time zones. I've loved it, but it's time for this to be over. Weeks of travel probably isn't for me. I really don't know how you do it.

Dixon: You get used to it after a while. It doesn't necessarily get easier, but it becomes routine.

Oscar: More than anything I can't wait to be in New York with you. It's going to be epic to see you play at the Garden, get our families together, and most of all, be home with you.

Dixon: Home. I like that word. My parents are so excited to see yours again. I think they're looking more forward to that than seeing you and me.

Oscar: I know it. My mom and your mom have been talking and they're organizing things to do in the city.

Dixon: My dad mentioned that. He thinks they're going to make up for all the time they didn't have their weekly get-together in those few days.

Oscar: Good for them.

Dixon: Right! We'd still be catching up even if we didn't fall for each other.

Dixon: I'm glad we didn't stay in the friend zone.

Oscar: Me too. This is so much better.

Dixon: We should talk about summer plans as soon as you get here, or even over dinner one night if you want. It seems far away. But I know it's going to get here fast. I'd love to figure out if we can take a trip. Or what we want to do if I'm going to be in Miami for a couple months. We've talked about showing off our favorite places, but what comes after that?

Oscar: A trip would be amazing, and a lot different than traveling around for work. There are so many places we could go and I know I could get a week off later in the summer. But I'd be happy to stay home too. As much as we've traveled this year, there might be something to being homebodies for a while.

Dixon: Very true. I'll have between two and three months, depending on how we do in the postseason.

Oscar: I haven't heard what the summer program is going to be, but typically I teach during the day and perform in some of the productions. There should be lots of options. I'll check on that before I come up there.

Dixon: Is it weird I enjoy talking about this everyday stuff?

Oscar: Nope. I love it too. Whatever we decide, we're going to have a great time because we're together. I actually look forward to being able to just hang out on the couch, watch a movie, and eat popcorn.

Dixon: Yes, please. Summer's not going to get here fast enough. At least we're both going to be plenty busy between now and then.

Oscar: It does pay to be busy.

Dixon: Speaking of busy, I gotta run. Being called to the ice for our skate. I'll ring you up after the game since we've got the team dinner tonight. Have a good show. I love you.

Oscar: Play good. Talk to you after. I love you too.

TWENTY-FIVE

DIXON

Oscar's tour had ended in Seattle at the end of last week. Giddy anticipation summed up my mood as Oscar's arrival day got closer.

Caleb, Dimitri, Cole, and some of my other teammates had all commented over the course of the past few days about how much I fidgeted. If I was sitting somewhere, my leg would bounce. Standing on the ice listening to the coaches on strategies, I'd keep shifting position. The excitement of spending a couple of weeks with him had been increasing exponentially.

Luckily, the team loved it at game time when all the energy had a release. Excitement seemed to translate into serious game-time focus. I ended up racking up multiple points per game, especially assists, which gave my season stats a nice boost.

Oscar went to Miami for three days—enough time to check up on his place, check in with Miami Ballet, and pack to come north.

I played on the road while he was in Florida, which was good because I thought I'd have gone stir-crazy at home wanting to do something—anything—to make sure everything was perfect for his arrival. This despite the fact I'd already sorted all that out for his visit and our parents.

Each day we'd talk and text for hours, which was easy because I was playing on the East Coast, so no time zone calculations were needed. A home stint had aligned with his arrival, so we'd be able to spend a good amount of time together.

As a surprise, I'd decided to meet him at the airport. Since I lived downtown, I told him to fly into Newark since it made getting to my place easier.

I'd tracked his flight the whole way. It didn't matter that the weather was great in Miami and New York and along the flight path, I still checked relentlessly to make sure everything was good. Plus I wanted to be at the airport on time.

Along with the other people who were waiting, I planted myself where people would exit from the gates. I resisted the urge to buy a ticket so I could get through security and be there just as he came off the plane. That seemed ridiculous and clingier than I wanted to be.

Constantly refreshing the flight status finally let me know the plane was at the gate.

Of course, at that point time slowed down. He had an exit row seat over the wing, so half the plane had to deplane before he could. I knew he had to come out this way even though he hadn't checked luggage, so the only risk was missing him in the crowd. I had a hunch, though, that the universe would make sure we'd find each other since we'd come this far.

My phone chimed the tone I'd assigned to Oscar.

Oscar: I'm here! Walking off the plane now. I'll let you know when I'm in a car and on my way.

Dixon: Great! Can't wait to see you.

I responded quickly but didn't let him in on the surprise even as I surveyed the crowd closely.

So many people streamed out from the automatic doors.

Suddenly it was like the sea parted and Oscar came into view. He had his usual backpack tossed over his shoulder as well as a roller bag next to him. His head was bobbing to whatever was playing through his headphones.

My focus locked onto him so I wouldn't lose him as I moved his way.

The double take he did when he saw me made my heart swell.

I stopped, smiled, and gave a small wave.

His eyes went extra wide and his smile was huge as he sped up, weaving his way through the throng of travelers.

The hug was one of the tightest ever and we kissed. We managed to keep it tame since we were at the airport, but it felt like something out of a movie as lovers reunited.

"You could've told me you were waiting." Oscar cocked one eyebrow as he liked to do and wrapped an arm around mine to link us together. He kept hold of his pack with his free hand, and I took his bag.

"Where's the fun in that? The look you had when you saw me was priceless."

"I'm going to have to figure out a surprise for you so I can see what your reaction is."

I took Oscar's hand in mine and headed for the parking garage. "I can't wait to see what kind of surprise you come up with. It know it'll be epic."

"Count on it."

On the way to the car, I got the ins and outs of the flight, including the noisy kid who managed to annoy everyone. Apparently, even Oscar's premium noise-canceling headphones couldn't completely drown the child out.

"I feel like I should be nervous about our parents coming in this weekend, but I'm not," Oscar said as I drove us into the city.

"Me either. If anything, my lack of anxiety sometimes makes me worried. Which I know is silly. I think it's going to be a great time, though. My parents are excited to get to see you and your fam."

"Same. Plus my folks haven't been here in a long time. They're making a whole thing out of it, doing more than we'd originally planned."

Since we'd already told them we were together so they'd hear it from us, the stress of that was already gone. Now it was just a celebration, which we planned for a big dinner on Saturday. Everyone would also come to my game on Sunday afternoon and then we'd have dinner again. My mom and dad planned to fly out Monday morning.

"How long did your parents decide to stay for?"

"They'll head home Wednesday morning. They're going to Carnegie Hall Tuesday night to see Audra McDonald." Oscar laughed a bit as he talked. "My dad's so excited he made that happen because Mom loves her. Anyway, they said they'd be good on their own the extra days. They don't want to cut in on my vacation and time with you."

As we approached my car, I triggered the hatch to open. "This is going to be a great weekend. And you may even get more time with your family."

"Maybe. Time with you is the most important thing." Oscar took off his backpack and stored it while I put the bag in.

"You can certainly hang out with them while I'm at practice, or you can just chill. Whatever you want."

He closed the hatch and pulled me into an embrace. "I can't believe we're together and have more than a couple of hours." His soft kiss on my lips sent shudders through my body.

"I thought this day would never get here. I hope you still like me at the end of these two weeks."

Oscar dropped a hand from my back and smacked my butt. "Don't say things like that. If anything, I'm going to love you so much more. I already know I'm not going to want to leave."

We traded a few more kisses. "Let's get out of here. The sooner we're home, the sooner we can kiss all we want."

Oscar nodded and gave me a devilish smile as he released me.

Contentment flooded through me as we got into the car. Two weeks with my boyfriend was officially underway.

TWENTY-SIX

OSCAR

"This looks good." Dad looked over the top of the menu and grinned from where he sat next to Mom. "The huge pizza section reminds me of all the pizza we shoved in you boys after all the practices."

I'd suggested Osteria del Sogno because it was an upscale throwback to the places we'd frequented when we were neighbors. A smile tugged at the corners of my mouth because Dad had picked up on that right away.

Dix grinned from his position at the other end of the table. We were sitting with Dix and me at opposite ends and our parents facing each other. It was the perfect setup for conversation, but it made it impossible for me to randomly hold Dix's hand.

"This is one of Nate's favorite places, and he brought the cast here on our last night in the city. I knew it was the perfect place for this dinner."

"You know, I still can't believe you two found each

other the way you did," Dix's father said. "Who would've thought that could happen?"

We studied the menu for quite a while before deciding to get caprese skewers, a couple of pasta dishes, and two pizzas loaded with meats plus garlic bread. The moment the server poured the wine, Mom gently tapped on her glass with a fork.

"Cheers," Mom said. "To old friends back together." Everybody clinked their glasses together. Dix and I raised ours toward each other since we were too far apart to reach.

"Connecting with Oscar again has been one of the best things that's ever happened. I've never been with anyone who makes me as happy, settled, and comfortable as he does. The time we've spent together so far has been incredible, and I'm excited to discover what's next for us."

I raised my glass. "Cheers to us."

"Cheers," Dix said, glass in the air.

Our parents joined in, clinking their glasses together again.

"We're so happy for you both." Dix's mother took her husband's hand. "We've always wanted Dixon to find someone wonderful. If you two are as thick as thieves like you were when you were kids, you're going to be very happy together."

Dad raised his glass. "Cheers to that." And another round of glassware connecting. "You've been through the bad, that—"

"No, sir." I cut him off. "We don't talk about that. I

already had to deal with him recently. We're not bringing that into this happiness."

Dad gave me a single nod. "You're right." He made a show of clearing his throat. "Here's to wonderful times."

"Cheers!" everyone said together. Joy bubbled up from every corner of the table, punctuated by smiles and the clinking of glasses. It was so good to have all of us together again.

People at other tables looked over and tried to figure out what was going on with all the hugging and toasts. Luckily, this was NYC, so it didn't dissolve into random clapping or anyone trying to ask what was happening.

"How's it all going to work?" Mom asked the inevitable question we'd prepared for. It was a win that they'd been congratulatory for as many days as they had before they'd gotten to the practical matters.

"We're working on that." I figured I'd dive in first since it had been my mom who'd asked. "For now, we're living in two places and there'll be lots of calls and texts when we're not in the same place. Dix will probably spend a lot of this summer in Miami. And we'll figure out the fall."

"There are a lot of options depending on how we want things to work long term," Dix chimed in. I wondered if we'd made a mistake not rehearsing some of this, but so far so good. "We'll figure it out as we go."

"You're not thinking of leaving the team, are you?" Dix's father asked. We'd expected that to be the first question, so we hadn't been too far off. As a longtime

New York fan, he was proud Dix played for them and considered it the pinnacle of success for his son.

"Not right now. I already told my agent that I'd be open to a trade to Miami if it came up," Dix said, causing his father to frown. "And who knows what might happen when my contract's up in a couple of years. Right now it's about the status quo. Oscar's not leaving his position in Miami either."

"For sure," I added. "There's no need to rock our professional lives. We're both exactly where we want to be."

Dix's father gave a slight nod. "I had to ask. You're both in such different careers from anything that I have experience with. You're both smart. I know you'll make good choices."

Dixon put his arms around his mom and my dad, and it kind of felt like he was hugging the entire table. "We'll make the best choices we can. We had great parents to learn from. I think I speak for both of us when I say we'd like to have a relationship as strong as yours."

He'd said the perfect thing. I mouthed *love you* to him and he smiled in response. Meanwhile, our parents glowed under that praise and my mom even wiped a tear from her eye.

The conversation stopped as the server brought our appetizer and topped off our glasses.

That pause was only temporary as Dad got back to it. "I can't imagine spending so much time away from your mom. I guess technology makes it easier." His tone wavered between a statement and a question.

"It helps," Dix said. "Seeing each other while we talk is great. We'd rather be in the same place, but it's an okay substitute. We've gotten into a routine of sharing dinner most nights and always talking before bed. I think we'll always do something like that when one of us is away."

"I'd imagine your money will make travel a lot easier," Dix's mother said.

Mom grimaced and she took a drink. Her discomfort wasn't a surprise since my family avoided talking about money in public.

Dix and I hadn't had that discussion at all. It hadn't come up. Without a word, we'd fallen into a routine of taking turns paying for things when we were together. It'd started with the pancakes in New York and continued through the cities we'd connected in. Of course, he made more than I did, by a lot, I suspected. We'd need to sort it all out at some point, but I hadn't expected it to come up here.

"I suppose." Dix's brow knitted together, and he paused before speaking again. "We'll have to see how we want to spend and what we want to save for."

A surge of emotion welled up and my heart might have skipped a beat at Dix's causal use of the word "we." He didn't focus on the money or how much we each had. Instead, like everything else, it would be a conversation for us to have.

"It's going to be a summer of discussion for sure." I didn't want to leave him hanging with that. "We've got a lot to decide on before training camp begins for Dix in September."

"What's your summer typically look like, Oscar?" Dix's father asked.

"Usually teaching a few sessions a week in the same program that I went to as a kid. I also dance in some of the summer shows. The class and performance schedules come out next week."

"That's wonderful that you're working to bring up the next generation the same way you were."

"I enjoy it and I'm glad I get to do it. It makes me happy to work with kids who remind me of me in so many ways."

"Weren't you going to work with New York's youth program this summer?" Dix's father looked at him.

Dix's jaw tightened momentarily. "Nothing was finalized. And since I want to be in Miami, I've asked to be put in touch with Miami's program so that maybe I can coach there instead. Then we can both be teaching."

Dix's father looked like he was going to say more, but his mom spoke up.

"I'm sure wherever you coach this summer, the kids will love it."

Dix's mother arched an eyebrow, her gaze locking with her husband for a fleeting moment. He responded with a slight nod. I wondered if Dix and I would develop that kind of communication.

"Let's not ask these boys too many questions." She looked at her husband and over to my parents. "They have plenty of time to figure things out. How much did any of us think about the future when we first got together?"

"Some days I'm not sure I've got anything figured out," Mom said with a laugh.

"Right there with you, honey." Dad leaned into her, and they shared a quick kiss through their amusement.

Dix's parents laughed too, and his mother took his father's hand in hers.

I arched my eyebrows at Dix and received a relaxed smile back.

Once again, the server had good timing and arrived with a tray full of food, followed by someone else with a second tray.

As we settled into the meal, the conversation shifted into easier topics. We talked about Dix's upcoming game we'd be at and the difference between traveling with a show and for games. Once our parents started catching up with each other, Dix and I were, happily, no longer the center of attention.

Finding Dix again had brought me so much joy, and seeing our parents reunited was wonderful too.

TWENTY-SEVEN

DIXON

I REACHED for the remote and hit pause before a seventh episode of *Schitt's Creek* could start. Oscar fit cozily into my side, his head resting against my chest. His legs stretched out on the couch while mine rested on the coffee table. We wore sweatpants and T-shirts.

We'd found this comfortable spot shortly after we'd started the show and only budged when Oscar set the empty popcorn bowl on the table.

"I think my new favorite thing is sitting like this and watching the best show ever. It's perfect, especially since I can touch you anytime." To illustrate the point, Oscar caressed along my thigh.

I dropped my arm that had been along the back of the couch and adjusted so it was draped across his shoulder. I idly rubbed his chest and maybe, accidentally, brushed against his nipple. The slight shudder he made when I did that was irresistible.

"We certainly found comfortable fast." I kissed his

cheek and then the top of his head. I loved how his soft hair felt against the scruff of my beard.

"I can't believe how well it went with our parents. It was practically like our reconnection."

"Right? I didn't expect mine would stay longer just to hang out with yours. We became old news fast. And I'm okay with that."

We laughed. My parents had extended their stay and joined Oscar's family, including going to the concert. While they were at Carnegie Hall, Oscar had been at the Garden watching me rack up a couple of assists in a win.

"I've been thinking about the summer." Oscar craned his head up to look at me. "What would you think of helping me find a new place in Miami? Something that's ours. I'd already been thinking about moving to a bigger space, and with you coming, it's the right time. I can do some scouting and share listings with you. Once we find something we love, we can go for it. If we can sort it sooner than later, I can get moved in before you come down."

Every time we talked about the summer, I remembered what it was like to be in school, eager for the break to start. On the one hand, I didn't want to jinx the team. There were signs we were set up to bring the Cup back to New York. On the other hand, if the hockey gods deemed it wasn't going to be a repeat, I would gladly make an early trip south.

"That's a great idea," I said. "I'd love to find something together."

"Do you want to rent it with me? Have both our names on the lease?"

"I'd love that. And I can add you to the lease here too or find a place together up here so it's something we both picked." I paused for a moment since I had a big question. "What about maybe buying something in Miami?"

Oscar went into deep thought. A shadow of concentration passed over his features. If he'd had glasses, he'd have an incredible scholarly look. I gave him time, knowing he'd talk when he was ready.

"I'm totally into getting a place with you, rent or buy. Is Miami where we want to stay enough to buy? I'd been thinking about buying but wasn't sure that made sense right now."

"Even as I asked the question, I thought that too." I ruffled his curls as we talked. "There's no telling where our careers will take us. We should talk to somebody about the ins and outs of buying property. If we leave Florida, we can sell or maybe turn it into a rental."

Oscar nodded and adjusted so he was sitting cross-legged facing me. "I have no clue what the better choice is—investment, rental. I've never had a reason to know that."

I snorted. "Me either. It'll be fun to learn it together."

Oscar sighed and ran his hand through his curls. Again I waited, but after a moment I gave him a questioning look, hoping he'd say what was on his mind.

"I suppose we should have the money talk?" he said, more timidly than I was used to. "This is the first time I've been in a relationship looking seriously at a future. If we're buying or renting together and figuring out the rest, I guess we need to get into that."

"I'll be honest. I have a ridiculous amount of money." My exaggeration on "ridiculous" made Oscar snicker. "Seriously, though, my spending is low and I like to save. I know this apartment doesn't exactly make it look that way. This was one of the many listings the team gave me, and I liked it the best. I didn't take a lot of time deciding where to live."

"There's certainly nothing wrong with it." He made a sweeping motion with his arm. "I mean look at it."

"I know, right? But it's not really me. What I'd really like here is a brownstone in Brooklyn. Or maybe live outside the city altogether in a house with a yard." I reached out and took his hand. "Anyway, we can do whatever we want. If it's important to make it where we contribute equally to housing costs, I'm good with that. Or we can find exactly what we want and pool our resources in whatever way makes sense."

"Should I even ask what a ridiculous amount of money is?"

I didn't hesitate to tell him because sharing and honesty were key. "I earn one point two million a year. Right now, I have around four million between available cash, savings, and investments. I want to make sure I'm set when my career's over so that me and my family"—I squeezed his hand—"can do whatever we want."

Oscar's eyes bulged a bit, and I held back a laugh.

"Okay then." He ran a hand through his curls again. "I have about fifteen thousand that I've put together over the past decade or so for a down payment. There's retirement stuff too, but I don't know how much is there. I've been putting money in with every paycheck since I started getting them. Dad made sure I did that."

"That's good. It was my mom that made sure I got someone helping with money, starting with the first contract I signed. She made sure too that I got someone good who wouldn't try to run off with anything."

"That sounds like her."

I took his hand that I was already holding and wrapped it in both of mine. "I don't want you to feel… I don't know… weird, I guess might be the word… in any way because of the money I'm able to contribute."

"You know, I didn't even think about it until dinner the other night. So far, we've been splitting things up without even talking about it."

I nodded. That realization had hit me while we'd been in Dallas, and I appreciated that it had just naturally happened.

"I don't know the right answer for this. How much you make compared to me doesn't matter. I love you, not how much you've got. If we're going to buy something together, though, maybe we need to talk to someone who can make sure we're thinking about everything we should be."

"I like that idea. Maybe my money person can help or knows someone who can?"

We exchanged a look, acknowledging the importance of what we'd just discussed.

"I love you." Oscar pushed himself toward me and

planted a perfect kiss on my lips. "I love we can talk about this stuff without freaking each other out."

"Because we're meant to be."

Oscar moved with his usual fluid grace, positioning himself so that he straddled me. "Do you think about the time that we missed?"

"Sometimes. I wish we'd been able to stay in touch as friends so we'd have celebrated all the things we'd achieved over the years. From the relationship point of view, I don't think I was ready for that until now since I was so career focused, trying to get established." I looked away for a moment before I met his eyes again. "There was a bratty streak in my late teens too that I'm sure my parents would love to tell you about."

"Really?" Surprise laced his voice. "Bratty? You? I think I need to call your mom right now." His eyes flashed with mischief, and I grabbed onto his arm so he couldn't get up.

"No, you don't. That conversation needs to happen in person so I can add context. Plus if you're gonna get the dirt on me, you can be sure I'm asking your parents too. Is there a diva stint in your background? I've seen some of those Netflix shows set in ballet schools."

"Uh-huh. I see. Coming out with the big guns trying to compare me to characters on *Tiny Pretty Things* or *The Next Step*. My parents have no stories like that and neither do my classmates."

"So does that mean you were perfect and the teacher's pet?" I raised an eyebrow at him.

"Oh no. I *wanted* to be perfect. It always felt like I

was on the edge of losing my scholarship. I was sure I wasn't as good as everyone else."

He certainly didn't show that now. But, just because he was confident on stage now didn't mean he always was.

"No need to frown." He pushed the edges of my mouth up with his fingers, which made me chuckle. "It was a phase I went through. Meeting Tobias after I was out of school and a member of the company didn't help either. I saw a good therapist after all that, so no need to worry." I sighed dramatically. "And If you really want *all* the stories, you can meet my friends this summer."

"I would love to meet them."

"Although I doubt they would betray any serious information"—he paused and plastered a devilish grin on his face—"like if I was a brat."

My mouth dropped open as I feigned shock. Oscar, meanwhile, put a quick kiss on my nose and we both ended up laughing.

My heart raced from the sheer joy of this moment, silly and spontaneous. Exhilaration rolled over me at having this random, lighthearted conversation with Oscar. I ran my hands over his arms and back.

"Speaking of friends, do you want to meet my teammates while you're here? I don't want people to think I'm holding you hostage or anything."

"That'd be cool."

"I'll see what everybody thinks at that practice tomorrow. Then we can do it all over again when I get to Miami."

"In case I haven't said it enough, I love you." He rested his forehead against mine. "I love making plans with you."

I wrapped him in a slightly tighter hug and put my lips on his. We moved quickly from easygoing kissing to something hungrier. We'd end up naked soon, either on the couch or on the bed or somewhere in between. There were still places in the apartment we hadn't made out yet, and we wanted to try all of those before Oscar left next week.

EPILOGUE
OSCAR

Two Months Later

I hung out in one of my favorite spots. This house had a front porch that had caught my attention when I saw the listing. The second story provided the overhang, which was clad in white beadboard—a classic look in my opinion. The rails were simple white spindles spaced far enough apart that you could easily see through to the shrubs and flowers that grew in front.

My parents' house had had a great porch when we lived in Wisconsin. Dix and I had both had nice backyards, but our porch had stuck with me for years as the thing I missed about that house. There were many snack breaks taken there, and it had also been the place to play on rainy days.

Dix and I hadn't bought an overly big place. Neither of us was into having more house that we needed. It was perfect for the two of us, with three bedrooms, two and a half baths, a garage, and a modest yard. We still had a lot to do to turn it into a home—the bright yellow paint in the kitchen was a bit much.

After we'd researched, we decided investing in a house was the way to go. We'd hoped we'd find a house quickly, and luckily that had come true. We'd contributed equally to the down payment and did the same with the mortgage.

I'd moved in last week. I hadn't had much to move, but I brought a couch, a bed, and other basics that made it possible for us to live here.

What the house and I needed to be complete was him.

While I'd promised not to do any major shopping before Dix arrived, I did get two Adirondack chairs to put out. The porch faced south, so there was some afternoon sun, but it had enough cover so it was pleasant. It had already become my preferred place to relax at the end of the day.

Relaxing right now was difficult, though, and my leg bounced as I kept looking down the street for Dix's Lyft. Because he had so much stuff with him, I couldn't pick him up in my small car.

So I waited.

Dix had texted he was on the way and should arrive in about forty-five minutes. That would get him here in time for the sunset, which I'd shared with him the last three days via FaceTime. In person would be even better.

Finally, a car with a Lyft sticker on the windshield turned onto the street and then pulled into the driveway. Dix quickly emerged from the back. I leapt from my seat, took the steps in one leap, and bounded across the yard to him.

"Hey there, Mr. New Homeowner." I leaned in to kiss him, which he returned. Over the past few days, I'd met a couple of the neighbors as I moved in and I let them know my boyfriend would join me soon. I didn't know how robust the gossip network might be, but if they didn't know a gay couple had moved in, the kiss would broadcast it.

"It's great to finally see this in person. It's perfect. And please tell me we're just going to hang out and have dinner on the porch. I can already see why you love it out here so much."

I followed as he went to help the driver unload. I caught sight of the packed rear of the SUV through the windows.

"Wow. I didn't realize we'd left so much for you to bring." I reached in and pulled out a couple of bags.

"I added a few things since you left, but it didn't seem like this much until I was loading it into the car to leave this morning. The skycap was less than thrilled. Given how much the airline charged for it, they shouldn't be complaining."

We quickly got the luggage unloaded and Dix fist bumped the driver, who was a transplanted New York fan.

"He was great to talk with." Dix rolled luggage up the driveway with me. "He told me that he wondered if it really was me given the profile picture or if it was someone who looked like me with the same name. We had a good chat about why we got knocked out last round and thoughts on who would win between Pittsburgh and Vancouver."

"I love finding a driver who's fun to chat with. Makes the ride go so much faster."

"The conversation definitely kept me from constantly looking at the app to see how much longer it would be. So, what's on our agenda for tomorrow?"

"I don't have anything scheduled for tomorrow because I want us to get settled and comfortable." We set the first of the bags in the foyer and went back to the driveway for the rest. "Mom and Dad are insistent on throwing a housewarming a week from Saturday." I rolled my eyes. "I agreed to it because it was easier."

"I can imagine."

"I don't think you can. She's already texting me Pinterest boards for 'cute housewarming ideas.'" I made air quotes for emphasis.

"We can be ready in nine days, right?" Dix raised an eyebrow as he sounded skeptical.

"Worst case, we'll hide the unpacked boxes in the garage."

"That works." He lowered his voice to a whisper. "Is it okay that I'm looking forward to the unpacking and the party?"

"Maybe a little." I whispered back and gave him a smile. "And speaking of planning, did you get the details for the Vermont trip?"

"Read them on the plane actually. I'm excited we get to do that together."

In a great coincidence, we'd been invited to participate in a Pride festival in Vermont at the end of the month. The organizers had reached out to me and Nate to see if we'd perform our duet during in an evening of dance. Separately, a hockey player Dix knows from Seattle who runs a hockey camp there asked him to come coach and play in a charity game.

It was an easy yes for us.

"Our first Pride month together, and we get to celebrate in a great way."

We got everything inside and closed the door.

"Welcome home." I drew Dix close and kissed him good and proper.

"Maybe I should've let you carry me over the threshold," he said when he broke the kiss.

"We can have a do-over." I took a step back and opened the door.

He gave me his killer smile before grabbing my hand and bringing me outside.

"How about we just kick back and check out our new neighborhood? I feel like it's been go, go, go all day."

For a moment I thought he was going to have me do the carry-him thing, which I totally would have tried. After all, I knew how to lift people, though maybe not someone as big as Dix.

"I'd like that."

The sky was a gorgeous blue, and a pleasant breeze came across the porch. We were both in shorts and Dix was sporting a New York shirt, which I should probably remind him could get him in trouble down here. I wore one of my many Miami City Ballet shirts.

We dropped into the chairs. As if we'd done this a thousand times before, our hands joined together. I hadn't realized I'd put the chairs close enough to do that.

"I love you and I love our home." Dixon's voice sounded beyond content.

"I love you too. It's going to be an amazing summer as we settle in here."

We held each other's gaze for a moment and lapsed into a comfortable silence. We watched evening descend on the neighborhood. A couple of kids tossed a football around in a yard down the street. Cars passed back and forth, and several people walked dogs. We waved at people who waved at us.

We remained hand in hand as the peaceful atmosphere enveloped us, promising many more evenings just like this.

Hockey players have been at the center of my stories for years. It started back in 2009 with *Rivals*, which is the second story I wrote and the first that was published. Many hockey romances have followed, and the *Hockey Hearts* universe was officially established with *The Hockey Player's Heart* in 2018.

The *On Stage* series started with a short that once had the title of *Dancer and Sexy Big Man*, which originally came out in 2010. In a second, expanded edition, the story got the better title of *Dancing for Him*.

Skating Back to You was conceived as a crossover between the series because I wanted a hockey player to get their HEA with a performer. It was fun figuring out how Dixon and Oscar would connect while they were both on the road and living in different states.

This story originally appeared in the *Love is All Volume 4* charity anthology. I am grateful that the incredible Xio Axelrod invited me to be part of that volume alongside some other fantastic authors. Before I even finished the story, I knew there'd be an expanded version because I liked Dixon and Oscar so much.

Another aspect I enjoyed was bringing together characters from other books. Dixon plays for New York, so his captain is Caleb Carter, and he plays alongside Dimitri Stanislov (both from *The Hockey Player's Heart*) and Cole Ackerman (from *Taking a Shot at Love*). For Oscar, his dance partner on the *Ballet Strong* tour is Nate Mayer from *Dancing for Him*.

I'm happy these universes are now merged into one.

The pas de deux that Oscar and Nate perform is inspired by the ballet *Touché*, which had its world premiere as part of the American Ballet Theatre's virtual gala in November 2020. Dancers Calvin Royal III and João Menegussi brought the choreography of Christopher Rudd to live in a dance that's billed as "an intimate and beautiful journey through romance, exploring the themes of male love." Since its virtual premiere, *Touché* has gone on to be performed in front of audiences as part of ABT's repertory. If you ever get the chance to see it, I highly recommend it. It is stunning.

I also have to thank RegencyFan93. RegencyFan93 is a long time supporter of my books. She read this story when I serialized it on a subscription platform during the first half of 2024. The feedback was so valuable and I'm grateful for readers like her!

And I also thank you for reading Dixon and Oscar's story. I hope you enjoyed these two guys as much as I do.

***Hockey Hearts* Romance Series**

- *The Hockey Player's Heart* (co-written with Will Knauss)
- *The Hockey Player's Snow Day*
- *Keeping Kyle* (*A Hockey Allies Bachelor Bid Romance*)
- *Taking a Shot at Love*
- *Skating Back to You* (*A Hockey Hearts* and *On Stage* crossover)
- *Head in the Game*
- *Rivals*

***On Stage* Romance Series**

- *Dancing for Him*
- *Love's Opening Night*

More Romance

- *Bicycle Built for Two*
- *Room Service*
- *Somewhere on Mackinac*
- *Summer Heat*

Young Adult Titles

***Codename: Winger* series**

Available in ebook, paperback, and audiobook (narrated by Kirt Graves).

- *Tracker Hacker* (includes the bonus short story *A Very Winger Christmas*)
- *Schooled*
- *Audio Assault*
- *Netminder*

More Young Adult

Available in ebook, paperback, and audiobook (narrated by Jason Frazier)

- *Flipping for Him*

Non-Fiction

- *Content for Everyone: A Practical Guide for Creative Entrepreneurs to Produce Accessible and Usable Web Content* (co-written with Michele Lucchini)

Want to try something different from Jeff?

"Codename: Winger" is a Young Adult Thriller series about high school hockey player Theo Reese. Theo balances school, hockey, and a boyfriend while also being a computer whiz kid/secret agent.

NY Times Bestselling author TJ Klune says "A fun and intriguing adventure with fast-paced action and a delight-fully authentic voice in Theo. This curious YA novel reads like an old-school thriller. Part mystery, part thriller, and all heart."

The complete series is available in ebook, paperback and audiobook narrated by Kirt Graves.

Start Theo's adventures now with "Tacker Hacker."

ABOUT JEFF

Jeff Adams has written stories since he was in middle school and became a published author in 2009 when his first short stories were released. He writes gay romance and LGBTQ young adult fiction...and there's usually a hockey player at the center of the story.

Jeff lives in central California with his husband of more than twenty-five years, Will. Some of Jeff's favorite things include the musicals *Rent* and *[title of show]*, and the Detroit Red Wings and Pittsburgh Penguins hockey teams. Of course, he loves to read, but there isn't enough space to list out his favorite books.

In his day job, Jeff is a digital accessibility expert and he consults with companies around the world about making their digital experiences accessible. He's brought that knowledge to creative entrepreneurs with *Content for Everyone*, a book which helps creatives understand what they can do to create content that is accessible and usable by everyone.

Learn more about Jeff, his books at JeffAdams Writes.com. From the website you can also sign up for his newsletter to get a free novella from the *Hockey Hearts* universe, as well serialized stories, previews of new books, book recommendations, and more!